Anything But The Truth

by the same author

REWARD FOR A DEFECTOR
A PINCH OF SNUFF
THE JUROR
MENACES, MENACES
MURDER WITH MALICE
THE FATAL TRIP
CROOKED WOOD

ANYTHING BUT THE TRUTH

Michael Underwood

ST. MARTIN'S
NEW YORK

Library of Congress Catalog Card Number: 78–56355

Printed in Hong Kong

First published in the United States of America in 1978

ISBN: 0–31204522–0

Underwood

CHAPTER ONE

'I swear by Almighty God that the evidence I shall give shall be the truth, the whole truth and nothing but the truth.'

About as much hope of that, reflected Judge Matthew Chaytor, as finding icicles on the equator. He watched the witness put down the testament and the card from which he had just read the words of the oath in a thoroughly bored tone. He was a powerfully built young man, though not particularly tall. He had a neatly trimmed beard and a head of short-cut, curly brown hair which seemed to enhance the impression of a muscular physique.

His expression . . . Well, what with his facial hair and a pair of spectacles whose lenses were as opaque as treacle toffee, he had no visible expression. It was only assumption that he even had a pair of eyes.

Matthew Chaytor had been a judge for less than a year and this was the first time he had been called upon to sit at the Old Bailey. Moreover, this was his first case in his stint of duty there. He had known that, as a temporary, he'd be likely to be assigned the more commonplace cases to try, but that didn't mean he had to abandon any standards. And one of these was the importance he placed on the jury being able to observe the demeanour of a witness while he was giving his evidence.

Prosecuting counsel was about to begin his examination-in-chief when Judge Chaytor spoke.

'Just one moment, Mr Ridge.' Then turning to the witness, he said, 'Do you need to wear those dark glasses in court, Mr Cox? You won't find that there's any glare in here.'

He sensed rather than observed the witness's surprise. But it was only momentary.

'I always wear 'em,' the witness replied in a tone which effectively told the judge to mind his own business.

'Do you wear them on medical grounds?' Judge Chaytor asked with polite persistence.

The witness frowned. That much could be seen. 'Yes,' he replied, curtly.

'On doctor's advice?'

This time the witness paused before answering and slid the tip of his tongue across his lips.

'I don't see what it's got to do with anyone whether I wear 'em or not.'

'It's just that the jury can't observe you as well as they might. It's rather as if you were wearing a mask.'

'They can hear me all right, can't they?' the witness enquired truculently.

'Very well, if you wish to keep them on, I certainly can't force you to take them off.' Matthew Chaytor turned back to prosecuting counsel. 'Yes, go ahead, Mr Ridge.'

'Is your name William Cox?' counsel now asked.

'No, it isn't.'

Mr Ridge gave a nervous start. 'What is your name, then?' he asked anxiously.

'Billy Cox.'

'You mean you were baptised Billy, rather than William?'

'I mean my name's Billy Cox. I've never been called William in my life.'

Mr Ridge, who was young, intensely serious and relatively inexperienced, glanced worriedly at the judge. He seemed to feel that his whole case had been undermined before it had begun.

'Do you wish me to pursue the matter further, my lord?'

'In what way, Mr Ridge?'

6

'Over the question of his name, my lord,' counsel replied in a strangulated tone.

Matthew Chaytor wondered whether he had ever sounded so feeble when he was a young barrister. In the event, he gave prosecuting counsel the benefit of the doubt and smothered the tart retort he was minded to make.

'I suggest you get on with your examination of the witness,' he said, in a not unkindly tone. Apart from anything else, he had already formed the view that it was the first and last wholly truthful answer they were likely to hear from the bearded, blacked-out Billy Cox.

The person at the centre of this forensic flurry had followed the exchanges with the same wary and frowning expression he had worn since his trial began. His name was Ian Tanner and he was nineteen years old. Unlike the witness in the box, Tanner's face reflected every change of emotion, though he sat, for the most part, with a worried, slightly resentful, look which, from time to time, lapsed into plain boredom.

The prosecution's case hadn't got far and Billy Cox was the first important witness to testify. Tanner now glanced at Andrew Batchford, his own counsel, who was doodling on the cover of his notebook. He seemed to spend a lot of time doing so and, from a distance, the doodle gave the appearance of rampant ivy spreading over a wall. Tanner gazed at the row of faces in the public gallery and wished that his girl-friend was there to give him a reassuring smile. But Gail was to be called as a witness for him and so was not allowed into court before giving her evidence. She had stood by him from the beginning. From the moment he had arrived at her flat in a blind panic and told her in halting phrases what had happened. Six months had passed, but the memory of that September evening was burnt into his mind.

He could still see her expression of burgeoning alarm as he had burst in. She had been expecting him, of course;

7

but not out of breath, dishevelled and as if all the forces of hell were on his heels.

'What's happened, Ian?' she had asked as he had flung himself on to the settee, and begun to shake as if a pair of giant unseen hands had seized him.

'I've had an accident,' he blurted out. 'I think I've killed a bloke. You've got to help me, Gail.'

'Where's your bike now?' she asked, trying to make her voice sound calm. She had always known that one day he would come to grief on his motor-cycle. He rode too fast, determined to show off his prowess. She had felt herself in competition with the yellow monster from the outset and had resented its intrusion into his life. If it was now a mass of twisted metal, she was secretly pleased. But such a hope was stillborn.

'I wasn't on my bike,' he said with a tortured groan, 'I was in a car.'

'A car? What car?'

He bit his lip. 'I'd taken it for a sort of lark. Well, we had, that is.'

'Who was with you?'

He shook his head in misery. 'I was alone, but it was Mick's and Gino's idea as well.'

'How do you know you killed someone?'

'I must have done. I hit him smack on as I came round a bend. His body sailed right over the top of the car and landed behind.' He succumbed to a further bout of violent shaking. 'It was awful,' he went on in a choked voice, 'I can still hear the sound in my ears. It was a horrible sort of soft thud.'

'Did you stop?'

He shook his head. 'I just ditched the car and came here as quickly as I could.'

'Did anyone see the accident?' she asked in the same gently persuasive tone.

'They can't have done. It was down a lane. There was

no one about. No one, apart from this bloke who just lurched into the road as I came round the bend.'

'He must have been drunk,' Gail remarked thoughtfully.

Tanner nodded. 'Yes, that's it, he must have been. I hadn't thought of that,' he said seizing on her note of hope like a shipwrecked sailor grasping a lifeline.

'In which case it wasn't your fault. And, anyway, he mayn't be dead. Probably he's only injured.' She paused. 'You haven't said whose car you were driving, Ian. But I'll make some coffee and then you can tell me the whole story and we can decide what to do.'

'I could do with a coffee,' he said. He also needed time to think how much to tell her. Now that the initial onset of panic was receding, he must try and assess his situation.

Gail disappeared into the tiny kitchen of her flat which was situated above a ladies' hairdresser's salon in a quiet surburban street. The upstairs premises were shabby and in need of repair, but the rent was correspondingly low and she regarded herself as fortunate in having the privacy that many of her girl-friends lacked. By day she worked as a manicurist in the shop below.

By the time she returned with two mugs of coffee, Tanner had reached the conclusion that he could tell her everything except the real reason for having taken the car. She didn't need to know that in order to help him and it was better that she shouldn't. There were some things it was wiser not to tell a girl like Gail. During the six months they had known each other, he had come to rely on her in a good many ways, rather more than masculine vanity allowed him to admit. He was aware, however, that she took their relationship more seriously than he did. So far as he was concerned, she was no more than his current girl, even though she had lasted longer than most. But if she became too cloying, he wouldn't hesitate to give her the push. After all, you'd be crazy to let a bird tie you down when you were only nineteen.

9

He had first met her at the Monkes Tale; the same Monkes Tale which was the starting-point in this evening's disastrous chain of events.

He took a sip of coffee and grimaced.

'It's as hot as bloody molten lead,' he muttered.

'Have you any idea who it was you ran into?' she asked, ignoring his comment.

He shook his head. 'It'd all happened before I realised. I never had a chance. He shot out in front of the car.' He paused. 'I was going a fair speed. The law was after me.'

'The police?' Gail's tone had a fresh note of anxiety.

He nodded miserably. 'I'd crashed some lights at red and almost collided with a panda car. It gave chase. I think I threw them off, but I can't be sure.'

'Whose car were you driving, Ian?' she asked in a brittle voice.

'Jeff Jakobson's.'

'What, the man who owns the Monkes Tale?'

'Yes.'

'You told me he'd gone on holiday to Spain.'

'He has.'

'You mean, you just took his car?'

'Look, stop asking questions like a bloody barrister, will you! Yes, I took it.'

Gail bit her lip. 'I'm sorry, Ian. I didn't mean to nag. I was only trying to help you tell me what had happened.'

'O.K.,' he said in a mollified tone. He gave her hand a squeeze and she kept hold of his, gently massaging it with her fingertips. 'I took it for a lark, like I said. Well, it was more like a bet. We were in it together, even though I was the one who actually took it.'

'You mean, you, Gino and Mick?'

Gino Evans and Mick Burleigh were Ian's two closest mates and Gail didn't like either of them. In fact, her dislike of *them* was only equalled by her dislike of his motorcycle.

10

'You'd better phone Gino and find out what he knows. He was at the Monkes Tale when I left. He may have heard something. I don't want to talk to him in case the police are with him. They'll have found out where the car came from and some busybody may have given them my name.' He paused and frowned. 'Mick never turned up this evening. We were meant to meet at nine o'clock, but he never came.'

Gail glanced at the electric clock on the wall. It showed half past eleven. It seemed as if hours must have passed since Ian's arrival, but it had been little more than ten minutes ago that he had rattled her door with an urgency that had transmitted itself as clearly as if all the alarm bells in the street had suddenly begun to ring.

'Where's the car now?' she asked, quietly.

'I dumped it in the trees near the old pumping station in Waterworks Lane and scarpered on foot.'

It was Gail's turn to frown. Why had he been driving along Waterworks Lane? It didn't lead anywhere. It petered out where it emerged from the trees close to the now disused pumping station. After that, there was a stretch of rough grassland and on its farther side Prince's Farm Lane began and ran to a main thoroughfare. In effect, the two lanes and the piece of connecting grassland comprised a short cut between two residential areas on London's south-west fringe, though it was not used by anyone who valued his car, for the stretch of grassland was excessively bumpy when dry and inclined to become quickly waterlogged after rain.

So, Gail wondered, what on earth had Ian been doing driving along Waterworks Lane, if he had taken the car only for a lark, as he said? Then she remembered about the police being on his tail because he'd shot a red light. He must have been trying to throw them off. But instinct warned her against questioning him more closely about

11

this. She felt certain that he'd only shout at her again. For the moment she must restrain her curiosity.

She leaned over and gently stroked his forehead. Then she brought her head closer and kissed him on the mouth. His lips were dry and didn't respond. When she drew her head away, she saw that he had closed his eyes.

There were streaks of dirt on his face and he looked utterly exhausted – and vulnerable. He only needed to shave every other day and there was a faint growth of stubble on his chin and along his upper lip.

Cradling his head in the crook of her right arm, she lay back against the settee and let out a deep sigh. Some of her friends teased her about being a baby-snatcher, knowing that she was two years older than Ian. But this never bothered her. She recognised that he evoked some sort of maternal instinct in her. And why not! His real mother had deserted him when he was two, going off with a man and leaving her son to the care of the local authority. He knew even less about his father. Compassion apart, she was also genuinely fond of him, though she could do without his motor-cycle, his friends and certain of his moods. At times, he could be really nasty to her. Hostile, mocking and spiteful. Then he would as suddenly melt her by a show of vulnerability.

He now opened his eyes and stared at her gravely for a while. 'You are going to help me, aren't you, love?' he said in a whisper.

'Of course I am.'

'You could say that I spent the whole evening with you here?'

Gail gave him a puzzled look. 'What good would that be when people saw you at the Monkes Tale?'

'It could all be a question of times. We don't know yet. You might have to say that I arrived here earlier than I did. You wouldn't mind doing that for me, would you, love?'

Gail shook her head uncertainly. 'But if someone saw you take the car . . . And, anyway, the police in the panda car may have seen you and be able to recognise you.'

'Whose side are you on?' he asked, with a fresh edge to his tone.

'Yours, Ian, I really am. It's just that it mayn't be as easy as you seem to think. I mean, they may be able to trace you through fingerprints. Don't they always look for fingerprints on driving mirrors and steering-wheels?'

'Christ! I hadn't thought of that.' He looked so dashed that Gail started gently stroking his forehead again. 'Oh, God, why didn't I give everything a wipe? I was going to, but then the accident put it out of my head.'

'That's hardly surprising,' she said in a soothing voice.

But he didn't appear to be listening and a second later he visibly brightened. 'That's it. That's what I'll say if they get on to me. I'll tell them I don't remember any accident. That my mind's a blank. And you can say that when I arrived here I was completely dazed. I'd obviously had a terrible shock and you were very worried about me.'

Gail nodded dubiously. The truth was that she didn't really see how this would help him, but she hesitated to say so. At the moment, he was in no mood to be contradicted. Come to that, he never was.

'I'll say how this bloke shot out in front of the car giving me no chance to avoid him and that, as a result of the shock I suffered, I don't remember what happened afterwards.'

To Gail it sounded horribly implausible, but fortunately he didn't seem to be waiting for her reaction.

He reached for his mug of coffee. 'Better phone Gino. He's bound to be home by now.'

'What do you want me to say to him?'

'Find out what he knows.'

'Shall I tell him you're here?'

'Christ, no! At least not until you know it's safe. You'll

13

have to play it by ear. You know, find out if he's alone. If he is, I'll speak to him. I just want you to make the contact. O.K.?'

Gail walked across the room to where the telephone rested on a window sill.

'What's his number?' she asked unhappily. He gave it to her and she began to dial. 'Is that you Gino. It's Gail . . . yes, he is . . .'

She got no further, but, as Ian watched, her expression changed from hesitancy to utter dismay.

'Yes, I'll tell him,' she said half a minute later in a barely audible whisper and slowly put back the receiver. She turned and looked at Ian. 'He's coming round straight away.' Then in a bewildered tone she added, 'It was Mick Burleigh you ran into. He's dead.'

CHAPTER TWO

Mr Ridge gave his gown a fussed hitch and faced the witness with the expression of a nervous supplicant.

'Mr Cox, will you please tell the court what you were doing on the evening of Friday, the second of September last?'

Matthew Chaytor let out a silent groan. It was the sort of inept question that could plunge them all into an embattled situation before you could draw a second breath. He held his own as he awaited the reply. He never liked interrupting counsel and was aware of the danger of compounding confusion rather than removing it. But if necessary . . .

'I went to the Monkes Tale.'

Prosecuting counsel and judge let out their individual sighs of relief.

'Is that a roadhouse not far from Epsom?'

'S'right.'

'What time did you leave there?'

'About half past eight.'

'And what did you do then?'

'Went home.'

'Oh! And after that?'

'You want it blow by blow like?'

'No, we don't, Mr Cox,' the judge broke in quickly. 'You've come to court to tell us what you know of an accident that took place that night, so will you direct your mind to that. Mr Ridge, your questions are meant to elicit the witness' evidence, not roam over his life history.'

'My lord, I was trying not to lead,' prosecuting counsel said in a huffed tone.

15

'Yes, but keep to what is relevant, will you?'

Mr Ridge gave his gown another hitch, this time with a rather more petulant gesture and once more addressed the witness.

'My lord has helpfully referred to an accident that took place that night. Did you witness it?'

'No.'

'You didn't?'

'No. It happened round the bend.'

'Yes, of course,' prosecuting counsel said with a fresh surge of relief. 'Will you please tell my lord and the jury what you know about it.'

'I was walking along this lane when I heard a car coming up behind me. Its engine was revving like crazy and I nipped into the ditch on my left just in time. It shot past and disappeared round a bend just ahead and then I heard a terrific bang. I ran along the lane and there was this body lying in the middle of the road.'

'What did you do?'

'I stooped down, but I could tell the poor guy was dead. He was lying there like a heap of old clothes.'

'And then?'

'I was still kneeling beside the body when another car came round the bend. I thought it was going to run over us both, but it managed to brake in time and a couple of policemen got out.'

'They were in a panda car?'

'S'right.'

'And did you tell them what had happened?'

'Yes.'

'After the first car had passed you and gone round the bend, did you ever see it again?'

'No.'

'It didn't stop?'

'I could hear its engine screaming as it made off.'

'What time was this?' the judge asked.

'Around ten, I'd say.'

'Had you ever seen the victim before?'

'Yes.'

'Where?'

'At the Monkes Tale.'

'Did you know his name?'

'I'd heard someone call him Mick. I didn't know the rest of his name.'

'So you didn't know him well?'

'I'd never even spoken to him. He was just a young chap I'd seen there.'

'That's all I wish to ask this witness, my lord,' Mr Ridge said and sat down with apparent relief.

Andrew Batchford now rose to his feet. He had a smooth, moonlike face and a small squashed nose on which were perched a pair of rimless spectacles. He had reached an age which clients like Ian Tanner regarded as irretrievably ancient, whereas most of the judges before whom he appeared would still refer to him as young Batchford. Behind his impassive exterior lurked a sharp mind and a tolerant regard of most human foibles.

For a few seconds he stared mildly at the witness on the other side of the court.

'Tell me, Mr Cox, were you wearing those dark glasses on the night of the accident?'

'No.'

'Not?' The tone was fairly mocking.

'It was dark, wasn't it?'

'So you don't wear them after dark?'

'No. But they were in my pocket.'

'In case you suddenly ran into light, perhaps?'

Billy Cox's brow creased in an angry scowl, but he made no reply and, after a brief pause, defending counsel went on.

'What were you doing in Waterworks Lane at the time?'

'What d'you mean, what was I doing?'

17

'It's a simple enough question, isn't it? Well?'

'I was on my way to visit my girl.'

'On foot?'

'Yes, because my car was out of action.' There was no mistaking the note of triumph in Billy Cox's voice.

'Where did your girl live?'

'At the other end of Prince's Farm Road.'

'What's her name?'

'I won't say.'

'Why not?'

'Because she has a husband,' Cox said grudgingly.

'I see. Well, I won't press you about that at the moment. Tell me this, were you able to see the face of the driver of the car?'

For a second the witness seemed to hesitate and then he said, 'No.'

'But you did know the defendant by sight?'

'I think I may have seen him at the Monkes Tale a few times.'

'With Mick Burleigh, perhaps?'

'I don't remember who he was with.'

'Have you seen him there since the accident?'

'I don't think so.'

'Did you recognise the car as it went past?'

'I could see it was a Ford Granada.'

'But did you recognise it as Mr Jakobson's?'

'No. Didn't have time to see things like that. If I hadn't dived into the ditch real quick, I'd have been a corpse as well.'

'Was it being driven on headlights?'

'No, it wasn't.'

'Are you sure?'

' 'Course I'm sure.'

'My client will say that he did have his headlights on in the dipped position.'

'He can say what he likes. I'm telling you he didn't.'

18

'Do you think he ought to have spotted you?'

The witness gave a shrug of indifference. 'I don't know whether he saw me or not. I saw him all right.'

'But you've just said that you didn't see him?'

'I didn't see his face, but I saw the car all right,' Billy Cox said vehemently.

'Did you ever get to your lady friend's house that night?'

'No. By the time the police had finished with me, it was too late.'

'Were you quite happy to give the police a statement?'

'What d'you mean happy?'

'You weren't reluctant to become involved as a witness?'

'I'd as good as seen this young chap killed. It was my duty to help the police.'

'Do you always behave so commendably?'

'I don't know what you mean.'

'Nor do I, Mr Batchford,' the judge broke in.

Andrew Batchford blinked. What he was trying to impart to the jury was that the witness was not the socially conscious citizen he appeared to be. He knew that Billy Cox had seen the inside of prison on a couple of occasions. Unfortunately, Ian Tanner had also been inside and he couldn't impugn the witness' character without his client's record also being put in evidence. It wasn't so much that Tanner had been to Borstal for house-breaking as that he had a couple of convictions for speeding.

'I'm sorry, my lord, I withdraw my question.'

'It seemed to me more an observation that a question, Mr Batchford.'

'Then I withdraw my observation, my lord,' defending counsel said placably.

It was at this point that Temporary Detective Constable Patrick Bramley hastily smothered a cavernous yawn. It was his second in as many minutes and he had become suddenly aware of the judge watching him during the first unsmothered one.

19

The case had been largely prepared by the uniformed branch of the local station and T.D.C. Bramley had come into it only at the last minute, being told to go along to court as the officer nominally in charge. In effect, to act as general dogsbody and be on hand to assist prosecuting counsel with any queries.

He had read the file without finding anything in it to arouse his interest. There seldom was in traffic cases; even where a death was involved. At least, the court was warm and dry which was a change from standing in the rain keeping lengthy observation on someone's premises.

Though he had volunteered for work in the C.I.D., it hadn't been long before disillusionment had crept in. The irregular, not to mention unsocial, hours led to constant bickering with his girl-friend, Jennie, who resented the disruption of their social life.

Several times he had been on the verge of tendering his resignation and seeking a steady nine-to-five job. But Jennie had never reached the point of delivering an ultimatum and so he hadn't yet been forced into taking a decision. The truth was that the original appeal of a career in the police, though diminished, had never become completely extinguished. So just when he thought he was all ready to chuck it in, he would feel an unmistakable tug the other way and would decide to hang on a bit longer.

He felt a sudden prod in his back and turned to find out what prosecuting counsel wanted. His estimation of Mr Ridge was no higher than anyone else's. Pathetic it was, the way cases could be lost through counsel's ineptitude. Some hapless police officer toiled his guts out to build up a strong case, only to see counsel throwing great chunks of it out of the window. A lot of counsel were very good, a whole lot more were adequate, but there were still enough lousy ones to make you weep.

'Let me know as soon as the pathologist arrives,' Mr

Ridge hissed. 'Then I'll call him and ask for his release. I expect he'll want to get away.'

'He's been here for half an hour, sir,' Bramley retorted. 'That's him sitting over there.'

By tradition, professional witnesses such as doctors were usually allowed to sit in court while waiting to give their evidence. The defence could, however, always ask that they be excluded in the same way as other witnesses.

'You should have told me,' Mr Ridge said petulantly.

'I assumed you knew him by sight, sir,' Bramley replied in a tone that was anything but contrite.

The small altercation over, he turned his attention to Billy Cox who was still in the witness box. It was funny seeing a villain like Cox giving evidence for the prosecution, though it was doubtful whether *he* found it funny. Bramley was sure that Cox would have avoided the experience if he possibly could have. But having been caught at the scene by the police, he had had no effective choice in the matter.

Bramley knew from C.I.D. talk that Billy Cox was a member of the Sweetman gang whose nucleus comprised Totty Sweetman, Ron Hitching and Cox, with Totty's wife, Pauline, more than a mere camp follower. They were believed to have been responsible for a number of recent robberies and burglaries in the area, but so far they had managed to escape arrest. It was the familiar story of the chasm that always exists between suspicion and evidence.

Cox had certainly demonstrated that he was a cool customer. The way he had stood up to the judge and refused to remove his sun-glasses, you had to respect him. Not that judges were what they used to be! There weren't many left who could still strike cold terror into anyone incurring their displeasure. On the whole, Patrick Bramley considered that to be a good thing.

He turned his head to look at Tanner who was leaning forward and staring at Cox with an expression in which anger, fear and puzzlement all manifested themselves. At least, reflected Bramley, he had mown down one of his own ilk. Far better that than some innocent old age pensioner on his way home from bingo.

Half a minute later, Andrew Batchford completed his cross-examination, which, he would have been the first to admit, had got him almost nowhere. Just as you can't make bricks without straw, so you cannot cross-examine without material, and Tanner had provided him with virtually none. Moreover, he had been unable to detect any obvious chinks in Cox's evidence which could be profitably exploited.

Mr Ridge announced that he would now call Dr Butterworth, the pathologist.

The doctor stepped lightly into the witness-box, took the oath in a brisk tone, opened a buff folder on the ledge in front of him and glanced at prosecuting counsel as if to cue him to start asking questions.

It was a full minute, however, before Mr Ridge finished shuffling his papers as he sought to find his place.

'What is your full name, Doctor?'

'Alistair Robert McFee Butterworth.'

'And are you a registered medical practitioner and a pathologist?'

'I am.'

'And do you hold degrees from many universities?'

Judge Chaytor broke in. 'Dr Butterworth's is a household name, Mr Ridge, and I don't think we need list all his distinguished qualifications. Let's get on with his evidence.'

Prosecuting counsel pouted and seemed about to argue, but finally thought better of it.

'On the third of September last year did you perform a post-mortem examination on the body of Michael Burleigh?'

'I did.'

22

'What did you find?'

'I found the body of a healthy, well-nourished young man. He had a small scar on the right side of the lower abdomen indicating an appendectomy, that is an operation for appendicitis, some years ago. Apart from that, there was no evidence of any natural disease in the body. His death had resulted from multiple injuries, consistent with his having been struck by a vehicle travelling at considerable speed.'

Dr Butterworth looked up from his notes and peered at the judge and both counsel over the top of his spectacles as if to assure himself that they were paying attention. Mr Ridge, for his part, was clearly basking in the reflected glory of a witness whose evidence came forth without the use of a tin-opener. Not that it would have occurred to prosecuting counsel that he was other than sharp and effective in examining witnesses.

'At what speed would you estimate the car to have been travelling to have caused such injuries?'

The pathologist gave a small frown of annoyance. 'I can't possibly answer in terms of miles per hour, if that's what you mean.'

'Oh!' Mr Ridge said in an abashed tone. 'Then I haven't any further questions to ask you.'

Matthew Chaytor sighed. It was a rather histrionic sigh which he immediately regretted. He didn't want to acquire a reputation for having succumbed to an early attack of judgitis. But why should he have to do counsel's work for him!

'I think the jury would probably like to have some details of the multiple injuries of which you have spoken, Dr Butterworth. Perhaps you'd describe the major injuries you found.'

'Certainly, my lord. The most serious injuries were a ruptured aorta, that is the main artery which carries blood from the heart, and a ruptured spleen. Either of those injuries was sufficient to have caused death. There was also gross damage to the liver and a fracture to the right thigh and to the right wrist. There was a hairline fracture of the skull in the right frontal area and some contusion to the brain underlying the fracture. The whole body was a mass of bruises and abrasions.' He glanced up. 'Is that sufficient detail, my lord?'

'Yes, thank you.' The judge's brow became furrowed in thought. After a pause, he asked, 'Can you say the sequence in which the injuries were sustained?'

Dr Butterworth pursed his lips. 'My surmise would be that the head injuries were caused when he landed in the road after being catapulted over the top of the car. The internal injuries I have described would have been caused when the vehicle struck him.'

'Which way was he facing at the moment of impact?'

Dr Butterworth re-pursed his lips. 'He was certainly not struck from behind,' he said thoughtfully. 'My inference would be that he was facing the oncoming vehicle, but probably at a slight angle. As I say, he didn't have his back to it when struck, that's quite definite.'

As this piece of evidence emerged, several members of the jury turned to glance at Tanner who sat scowling. The truth was that he was feeling scared, more scared than at any time since it happened. The combined effect of Billy Cox and the pathologist had been to make him sound almost like a murderer. The murderer, moreover, of one of his mates. Though what Mick Burleigh had been doing in Waterworks Lane that night still remained a mystery six months later.

'There's only one further question I'd like to ask,' the judge now went on. 'I'm sure the jury will have been wondering what evidence there was of alcohol in the deceased's body?'

A number of jurors nodded owlishly.

'None, my lord,' Dr Butterworth replied promptly. 'I

naturally obtained blood and urine samples. but analysis revealed no evidence of alcohol in either. Nor, I may add, of any drug.'

'Thank you, Dr Butterworth. Yes, Mr Batchford, you wish to cross-examine?'

Andrew Batchford rose resignedly to his feet, aware that the judge's questions had made his own task more difficult. Not that it would have been any easier if prosecuting counsel had done his job properly. For a few seconds, he gazed thoughtfully at the witness who stared back at him with an expression of confident superiority.

'I take it, Dr Butterworth, that you'd expect to find grave injury to anyone struck head-on by a moving vehicle?'

The pathologist gave him a small wintry, but knowing, smile. 'The extent of the injuries would depend on the force of the impact, which, in this context, means the speed of the vehicle.'

'But would you not agree that someone struck by a car going at, say, twenty miles an hour would be likely to sustain serious injury?'

'That would depend on how the person was struck.'

'I'm sorry if I didn't make myself clear,' Batchford said silkily. 'I was referring to someone struck head-on as was the victim in this case. I'm not talking about glancing blows.' Dr Butterworth frowned portentously. He didn't like being mocked by counsel, particularly by one of whom he had never heard before.

'I'd have thought it was self-evident that the greater the speed, the fiercer the impact, the more serious the injuries sustained.' His tone implied that he was used to giving lessons in simple logic to members of the legal profession.

But Andrew Batchford appeared unmoved.

'Would someone struck by a car going at a hundred miles an hour suffer worse injury than if the car had been travelling at only eighty miles an hour?'

25

After a slight pause, the witness turned to the judge and said loftily, 'Does the court wish me to answer such a hypothetical question?'

'Well, Mr Batchford?' asked the judge.

'Dr Butterworth is a forensic pathologist of great experience, my lord, and he has told the court that the car which struck the deceased must have been travelling at considerable speed. I am merely trying to find out what sort of speed he has in mind.'

'Considerable speed,' Dr Butterworth repeated tartly.

'Fifty miles an hour?'

'Possibly. Possibly more.'

'Possibly less? What about forty?'

'I can't exclude that.'

'What about thirty?'

'You are trying to push me into a corner, sir, and I decline to be so pushed,' the pathologist said severely.

Andrew Batchford shook his head sadly as though nothing was farther from his mind.

'Isn't it a fact, Dr Butterworth,' he said with an air of finality, 'that the injuries you've described were just as consistent with the victim having been struck by a car travelling at thirty miles an hour as by one going faster than that?'

'I have said that, in my view, the car must have been travelling at a considerable speed and I abide by that answer.'

The next witness was the expert who had examined the car and who testified to finding the nearside wing heavily dented, as well as shattered lights on that side. He had also found a fragment of the deceased's trousers caught in the bumper bar on the car's nearside.

He was followed by Jeff Jakobson who described himself as proprietor of the Monkes Tale. He was a heavily built man of around forty-five with thinning hair on top. The sort of customer to whom trendy barbers would immediately try and sell a discreet hairpiece. He sported a luxuriant moustache and a yellow rose in the buttonhole of his blue suit. Beneath an ingratiating exterior, he gave the impression of being ill at ease.

So far as the prosecution was concerned, his evidence consisted of saying that he had left his Ford Granada in a corner of the Monkes Tale car park when he went off to Spain on holiday and that he had not given anyone permission to drive it in his absence.

He looked relieved when Mr Ridge sat down, but a fresh look of apprehension came over his face as he observed defending counsel rise to his feet.

'You've known the defendant for some time, have you not, Mr Jakobson?'

'For the best part of a year, I'd say, sir,' he replied in a tone overflowing with a desire to please.

'As a result of his patronising the Monkes Tale?'

'Quite so, sir, quite so.'

'He has never given you any trouble of any sort, has he?'

'Absolutely not, sir.'

'You've always got on well together?'

'Certainly. Never a cross word between us,' he said with a forced laugh.

'Which is probably more than you can say for some of your customers?'

'Alas, too true, sir.' Jakobson shook his head in apparent rueful recollection.

'Would it be fair to say that you've always shown a liking for him?'

'Always got on with him, sir. Never one to give me any trouble.'

'Yes, but have you not done him favours from time to time? For example, given him an occasional drink on the house?'

'Quite correct, sir.'

'And on one occasion, when he was in difficulties, did you lend him some money?'

'Very probably, sir, very probably.'

'Five pounds, I think it was.'

'I'm always pleased to help the young when I can. "Never refuse a helping hand" is my motto, sir.' He beamed anxiously round the court, gave his glistening brow a quick mop with his handkerchief.

Andrew Batchford nodded encouragingly, while wondering whether anyone was being taken in by such a display of bogus good nature.

'Is it fair to say that Tanner would sometimes come to you for advice?'

'Yes, always been ready to help them, sir.'

'Approaching you as a friend and a man of the world?'

'Quite so, sir.'

Defending counsel paused. Having prepared the ground, he was ready to make his assault.

'Given your relationship, Mr Jakobson, it would not have been unreasonable of Tanner to have taken your car in the belief that you wouldn't mind, would it?'

'Well, sir, I don't quite know about that,' Jakobson said jovially.

'But you weren't very annoyed, were you, when you heard what had happened?'

'It put me to a lot of trouble with my insurance company.'

'I'm sure it must have done. But if there'd been no accident, you wouldn't have minded, would you?'

'I'd certainly have told him it was a naughty thing to have done.'

'But if you'd discovered on your return from Spain that he had taken your car for a short joy-ride and safely returned it, you wouldn't have reported the matter to the police, would you?'

'I don't expect I would have, sir,' Jakobson replied with the air of an indulgent uncle.

'Thank you, Mr Jakobson, you are being most fair,' defending counsel observed unblushingly, while the judge temporarily focused his gaze on the ceiling. 'I'd like now to ask you a few questions about the Monkes Tale.'

'Only too pleased to answer, sir.'

'I gather it's a roadhouse with a grill-room and a number of bars.'

'Correct, sir. Four bars to be exact.'

'Which bar did Tanner and his friends normally use?'

'The Knightes Bar, sir. That's K-N-I-G-H-T-E-S.'

'Are they all named after characters in the *Canterbury Tales*?'

Jakobson beamed. 'Indeed, sir. You could say that the whole establishment is dedicated to that great work of English literature. Scenes from it are depicted on the walls and some of the choicest dishes in the grill-room are named after its merry band of pilgrims.' His tone increased in enthusiasm as he went on, 'We serve a delicious soufflé, for example, which is dedicated to the Wife of Bath. It's one of our most popular specialities. I could tell you of others if you wished, sir.'

'I don't think you'd better tempt us further,' Andrew Batchford said quickly. 'Tell me this, what sort of person does the Knightes Bar cater for?'

'It's very popular with a certain class of clientele. It has a disco and a small dance floor. One can say that it's most favoured by the young and their friends.'

'So it's at the bottom end of the social scale of the various facilities on offer at your establishment?'

'You could put it that way, sir,' Jakobson said doubtfully. 'But when you say "bottom end", I trust you're not suggesting . . .'

'I'm not suggesting anything offensive at all.'

'I'm grateful to you, sir, for making that clear.'

29

'Thank you, Mr Jakobson, I have no further questions I wish to ask.'

When the court adjourned for the day, Ian Tanner was released on bail to appear the next morning. He had been on bail, apart from an overnight stay in a police cell, since being charged with causing Mick Burleigh's death by reckless driving and with taking and driving away Jeff Jakobson's car without the owner's consent. These were the two charges on which he was now standing trial.

The clerk from his solicitor's office, who had been in court notionally instructing defending counsel, but in fact surreptitiously reading a book on astrology, a subject which interested him far more than the law, came across to the door of the dock as Tanner stepped across the invisible line between custody and freedom.

'Better hang on a moment in case Mr Batchford wants to have a word with you,' the clerk said, nodding in the direction of counsel who was talking to T.D.C. Bramley.

'Is Jakobson known to the police?' Batchford asked casually as he gathered up his papers.

'He doesn't have any previous convictions, sir,' Patrick Bramley answered in a cautious tone.

'No, I know that.' Andrew Batchford smiled. 'It's only idle curiosity on my part. He's completed his evidence and is out of the case as far as I'm concerned, but he struck me as a pretty phoney sort of chap and I just wondered if he'd ever crossed your path.'

'I agree he's rather a dubious sort of character, sir,' Patrick said with the same note of caution.

'Ever been to the Monkes Tale yourself?' Batchford enquired, as he slipped a loop of pink tape round his brief.

'A couple of times, sir. But it's not really my sort of place. It's all a bit bogus.'

'Like its owner.'

They both laughed and Patrick went on, 'I went to a

dance there. My girl was keen to go. But give me a straight-forward pub any day.'

Andrew Batchford nodded and glanced across the court to where Tanner and the solicitor's clerk were hovering.

'Do you know anything about the background to the case?' he asked with a frown.

' 'Fraid not, sir. I've read the file, but that's about all. Seems reasonably straightforward on the face of it.'

'On the face of it, perhaps. Except that we're not seeing the real face, only a mask. Hasn't it struck you that way, too?'

'Frankly no, sir.'

'For your money, it's just another dreary traffic case?' Batchford said with a faint smile.

Patrick Bramley had the grace to blush, this being an accurate reflection of his thoughts.

Counsel picked up his brief and tucked it under his arm. 'This is no more than a charade we've been taking part in today. We've been told no more than what the witnesses have been willing to disclose, what they want us to believe. Take Cox and Jakobson. Don't let's fool ourselves that we've been extracting the truth out of them. Large parts still lie buried deep. Think about it!'

'Perhaps your client will uncover it when he gives evidence, sir,' Patrick remarked with a mischievous grin.

Andrew Batchford paused and turned back as he was walking away. 'That, if I may say so, is an extremely cynical observation.'

T.D.C. Bramley shoved his own papers into his brief-case and went off to attend to the sordid matter of sorting out witnesses' expenses. Defending counsel had left him thoughtful. The case did contain a number of unsolved mysteries when you came to think about it. It might be worth trying to dig away at them to find out what lay beneath. If only in the hope of relieving some of the bore-dom of the case.

31

CHAPTER THREE

Gail was waiting for Ian when he came out of court.

'Come on, let's get out of this building,' he said without pausing when he reached her.

She found herself trailing behind him as he strode purposefully toward the building's main exit. He shot across the road ahead of her, but did condescend to wait on the farther side.

'What's the rush, Ian?' she asked breathlessly when she came up to him.

'That place gets me down,' he said sourly. 'There were times when I felt like letting out a bloody great shout to stir them up. They're all a lot of bloody children dressed up in their stupid wigs and gowns and bowing to each other like it was a kid's game.'

'Was your barrister good?'

'Better than the other one. Anyone could tell *he* was useless. Got on the judge's wick, he did. I'd have given him the push if he'd been my mouthpiece.'

Gail shook her head incredulously. 'You'd think the police would pick the best.'

'I gather this bloke was a last minute substitute for the barrister who should have been there. They must have found him at the reject counter.'

They had not been back in Gail's flat for longer than fifteen minutes when Gino Evans arrived. He was a year and a half older than Tanner and the offspring of a Welsh father and an Italian mother.

'How'd it go today, Ian?' he enquired breezily as soon as he was through the door.

33

'You try sitting silent all day, with nothing to do except listen to other people yapping. It's bloody torture.'

'Don't forget I've done it, too.'

'Yes, but there were three of you in the dock.'

'So what! We couldn't talk. The warders glared if we so much as twitched an eyelash. Anyway, how'd it go?'

'How do I know? There's so much talk, it makes your head go round.'

Gino sighed. 'You're a fine one. It's your trial and you don't know how it's going. Did you speak to your barrister at the end?'

'Yes.'

'And what'd he say?'

'Just said he'd see me tomorrow.'

'Did you ask him how it was going?'

Tanner shook his head morosely. 'I wasn't in the mood, I was fed up.'

'What was Billy Cox like giving evidence?'

'He made out I'd been driving like hell.'

'I still don't understand how you never saw him, Ian.'

'He said he jumped into the ditch when he heard the car coming. Made out he'd only just avoided being hit himself. Said the car flashed past, went round the bend and then he heard the bump when I ran into Mick.' After a short silence, Tanner said edgily, 'What the hell was Mick doing in Waterworks Lane? You've been supposed to be finding out all these weeks and you haven't turned up a bleeding thing.'

Gino shook his head wearily. He knew that Ian was being provocative. On the other hand, he was ever mindful that it was Ian, and not he, Gino, who had the aggro of an Old Bailey trial. Their roles might so easily have been reversed. Indeed, they had been determined by nothing more weighty than the toss of a coin. In these circumstances, he was prepared to put up with Ian's spikiness

34

and show a degree of tolerance that wouldn't normally have been forthcoming.

'I'm still trying, Ian, honest I am, but it's been like swimming up a waterfall. All we know is that Mick never turned up at the Monkes Tale that night and that he didn't spend the previous one at home. He knew what the plan was. If he hadn't, he wouldn't have known to try and stop you in Waterworks Lane. Did prosecuting counsel put forward any theory?'

'He said that Mick and I were friends and that Mick had known about my going to take the car for a joy-ride, that he had been left behind and had taken a short cut to Waterworks Lane to stop the car there.'

'Quite neat. And, of course, it's correct that Mick knew you'd be in Waterworks Lane about that time. As a matter of fact, I don't suppose more than a couple of cars a week go along there at night. Just the odd courting couple.'

'Have you seen Mick's family again?'

'They're very uptight about what happened. His mum and dad still don't want to have anything to do with either of us. They seem to think we're to blame for his death.'

'We are in a sort of way. You as much as me.'

Gino bit his lip, but said nothing. Anything he might say would probably have the effect of provoking Ian into a fresh outburst and it was more a time for kid gloves. His expression, however, became suddenly thoughtful.

'I did learn something interesting a couple of days ago. Mick's sister, Tricia, used to be friendly with Ron Hitching. They broke up some time ago, but they were together when you had the accident.'

'Is that the Hitching who was one of Totty Sweetman's lot?'

'The same.'

'Well, what the hell are you waiting for, Gino? Why haven't you got on to her? What've you been doing these last two days, except sitting on your Italian fanny?'

'Give us a chance, Ian! I don't even know where she's living. She left three months ago. Had a row with her old man and walked out.'

At this moment, Gail returned to the room bearing a tray with two plates of sausages and chips and one of shredded cabbage and carrot with a sprinkling of grated cheese on top.

'Call that a meal?' Gino asked in a tone of disgust.

'It's all right, nobody's asking you to eat it; not that you couldn't do with a bit of weight-watching.'

Gino patted his stomach. 'It's all that lovely pasta.'

'Ian doesn't put on weight, whatever he eats,' she remarked, with a note of pride.

Ian now suddenly leapt up from the settee and, catching Gail round the waist, gave her a smacking kiss.

'Have that for starters. It'll give your rabbit food a bit of flavour.'

'What's made you so cheerful all of a sudden?' she asked.

'I just feel everything's going to turn out all right.'

Gino and Gail exchanged surprised glances behind his back.

Ian, meanwhile, sat down at the table and started to dig into his plate of food, disengaging one hand after the first mouthful to reach for the ketchup bottle. As the other two sat down, he said, 'I read the other day about some bloke who'd told the police he had been driving when he'd really been the passenger and they had to let him off.' He fixed them both with a triumphant look. 'That's what I'm going to say when I give evidence.'

'They'll want to know why you didn't say so before,' Gino said with a frown.

'Because I didn't want to get the real driver into trouble.'

'And who are you going to say was the real driver?' Gino enquired in a brittle tone.

'I'll say I don't know his name. I happened to meet him

36

casual-like as I was leaving the Monkes Tale and he offered me a ride home.'

'Why would you want to protect a bloke you'd never met before?'

'I'll . . . I'll . . . I'll say it was a friend, but I refuse to give his name.'

'That'll be as good as pointing the finger at me.'

'I know. But I won't mention your name and the police'll never get any evidence.'

'You'll never get away with it, Ian. Not at this late stage.'

'This bloke I read about did, so why shouldn't I give it a swing?'

Gail, who had been listening with a worried expression, laid down her fork and said, 'But what about your finger-prints on the steering wheel? How'll you explain them?'

'I'll say I had to get out on the driver's side and I clutched hold of the steering wheel. The passenger door was jammed, so I would have had to, wouldn't I?'

'But didn't Billy Cox say that the only person in the car was the driver?'

'Who's going to believe Billy Cox? He's a bloody liar. Anyway, I've thought of that. I'll say that I was so frightened by the way this bloke was driving that I was cowering right down and that's why no one could see a passenger.'

'You'll never get away with it, Ian,' Gino said in a robust tone.

'You're just worried about your own skin,' Tanner said viciously. 'It's been all right for you. I'm the one in the shit.'

'It won't help if you start to row,' Gail said quickly. 'What we need is a bit of calm thinking all round.'

'I've known people convicted just because they changed their story at the last moment.'

37

Tanner made a scoffing sound and Gail once more appealed for peace.

'You can say in your evidence, Gail, that you always felt I hadn't really been the driver.'

Over the past six months Gino had become such a frequent visitor to her flat that Gail had modified her opinion of him. She still didn't like him, but, in the words of the song, had grown accustomed to his face. However, her objection to Ian's new story was based solely on practical grounds and was in no way affected by Gino's anxiety about his own position.

Ian had told her how the three of them, that is he, Gino and Mick Burleigh, had tossed a coin to decide which of them should take Jeff Jakobson's car on a joy-ride. It had been one of those silly games of dare. One or two bits of the story didn't seem to her to fit, but she had ceased to worry about those and was ready to give evidence for Ian and back up his amnesia story. But now it seemed she was going to have to say something different to help him get out of his scrape.

She reached across for their empty plates and stacked them on top of her own.

'I'll make some coffee,' she said, 'and then we'll talk.'

'Got anything more to eat?' Gino asked sheepishly.

'A banana.'

'That all?' He made a face. 'O.K., I'll have a banana.'

While she was in the kitchen preparing the coffee, Ian and Gino sat in a prickly silence awaiting her return.

*   *   *

The Sweetmans lived in a 1930s semi-detached not far from the Kingston bypass and it was there that Billy Cox made for on leaving the Old Bailey.

The house had a deserted look, but he guessed that Pauline must be at home, probably in the kitchen preparing the evening meal. Their eldest child, Georgina, had recently started work and had an appetite as large as any boy's.

He rang the bell and heard movement inside. The door opened a crack and he glimpsed a small segment of Pauline's face.

'Oh, it's you, Billy,' she said, opening it fully.

'Expecting visitors?' he enquired as he stepped past her.

'No. But you never know. Jehovah's Witnesses, the law, nosy Mrs Grant from two doors down, they're all equally unwelcome.'

'Totty in?'

'He should be back in about half an hour. He's gone down to Horsham.' Cox raised a quizzical eyebrow and she added, 'He's heard of someone there who's interested in old silver. He decided to go and investigate, seeing that Percy's been put out of circulation.'

Percy was a well-known fence who had suffered the recent misfortune of being convicted of handling stolen property and of being sent to prison for three years. He had been bundled off, protesting vigorously that it was a trumped up charge. The truth was that an officer, who had long given him protection, had himself become the subject of a bribery enquiry. His successor had lost little time in obtaining a search warrant which had led inexorably to Percy's downfall. It had all happened so swiftly that Percy had only just caught his breath by the time he reached court and by then his fate was as good as settled.

'Where the hell's Horsham, anyway?' Cox asked.

'In Sussex, on the way to the coast. London's the only place you've ever heard of, isn't it, Billy boy?'

'It's the only one that matters.'

'Come in and I'll get you a cup of tea. Where've you blown from?'

'Come off it, Pauline,' he said in an affronted tone. 'I've been at the Old Bailey, haven't I?'

'The Old Bailey . . . Of course, now I remember.'

'Bloody well hope so.'

'How'd you get on?'

'O.K. Judge tried to get me to take off my sun-glasses, but I told him to get stuffed.'

'Some judges have a nerve! What happened to Tanner?'

'T'isn't over yet.'

'Totty still gets sore every time he thinks about it.'

'He should be more relaxed like me.'

'Wish he was. Not that I regard you as a model.'

'I know how to relax.'

'Perhaps you do, Billy, perhaps you do,' she said abstractedly. 'I worry about Totty.'

'No need to. He's O.K.'

'He's O.K. at the moment. But for how long?'

'What'd you mean?'

'How long before the law starts feeling his collar again?'

Cox made a scoffing sound. 'What's life but a few risks? Anyway, it's not like you to go soft.'

'I have not gone soft, Billy Cox,' she retorted sharply. 'It's just that I sometimes lie awake and worry about how it's all going to finish.'

'No mileage in that! It's like worrying about which maniac's going to drop an atom bomb on us. Nothing we can do about it, so it's better to forget it and get on with one's own bit of living. Does Totty know how you feel?'

'No, and don't you tell him!'

Cox grinned. 'That's more like the girl I know.'

'I suppose it's the kids I worry about most. Georgina's got a job in a surveyor's office and Clive's in his last year at school. It'd be much worse for them now if anything happened to Totty or me.'

'They'd survive.'

She gave him a disdainful look, but was saved further reaction by her husband's return.

'Billy's here,' she called out through the kitchen door.

Totty Sweetman was a couple of months short of his fortieth birthday, a big, heavyweight of a man. His black hair was streaked with grey and he had small, piercing eyes which gave him a permanently surly expression.

'How was Horsham?' Cox asked, as Sweetman flung his anorak on to a chair.

'Bloody waste of time!'

'What? He wasn't there?' his wife chipped in.

'Never found the bloody place. Drove around looking and asking, but he might have been a phantom for all I found out.'

'What've you been doing all day then?'

'Oh, I scouted around. It's a rich area. Could be some pickings to be had.'

'Don't expect Billy to go with you,' his wife said, throwing Cox a taunting look. 'Horsham could be in the Sahara for all he knows and cares.'

Sweetman digested the gibe in silence for a moment, then turning to his wife, he said, 'Give us a cup of tea, doll, and our Billy can tell me about Tanner.'

When Cox had finished, Sweetman, who had listened attentively, said, 'Did you speak to Jakobson afterwards?'

'No. Bit risky, I thought.'

'Are you going back tomorrow?'

Cox shook his head. 'No. I'm finished. I've been released.'

'Doesn't stop you going and listening.'

'It'd look funny. Might make someone get suspicious.'

'Perhaps it doesn't matter, anyway, seeing that nothing cropped up.' He held out his empty cup to his wife. 'Give us another, doll.' He remained silent until his cup had been replenished, then he said, 'Next item on the agenda is Ron Hitching. I'm not too happy about him.'

41

'I never have been.'

'Ron was O.K. until recently. But now it seems as if he's trying to avoid us. And I ask myself why he should be doing that.'

'He was friendly with Burleigh's sister.'

'We all know that! If he hadn't been, we wouldn't have found out what we did. He was on our side then, but is he now?'

The question was accompanied by a look of such piercing chill that even Billy Cox gave a small shiver.

'And take off those ruddy glasses. I can't see you properly.'

On this occasion, the offending sun-glasses were removed without demur and thrust into the breast pocket of his jacket.

*   *   *

Philippa Chaytor arrived home around five-thirty and immediately poured herself a small Scotch. Then she kicked off her shoes and put her feet up on the sofa.

She and Matthew had lived in the same house in Hampstead for over twenty years, during which time he had consolidated a busy and lucrative practice at the Bar and within the past year had been appointed to the Bench.

Being a judge's wife meant nothing to Philippa. She had always eschewed the social side of his career at the Bar and saw no cause to alter her ways now that he was on the Bench. Not that he expected her to do so.

She was fond of her husband and enjoyed his companionship more than anyone else's, but she had never shown more than a casual interest in his professional life. Indeed, he knew more of hers than she did of his, having been a director of the health-food shop she had founded until his judicial appointment obliged him to resign.

Though she now had a competent manageress in charge

of the shop, she still looked in several times a week. She continued to keep a close eye on the business side and travelled regularly in the ceaseless quest of satisfying new fads.

She was still stretched out on the sofa half an hour later when her husband came in.

'Had a bad day?' he enquired lightly, as he came into the room and saw her. Without waiting for a reply, he added, 'So have I!'

'What's been wrong with yours, Matt?'

'A dull case, an incompetent prosecuting counsel and a number of lying witnesses.'

'I'd have thought the lying witnesses should have livened it up.'

'That's being cynical.'

'I don't see how you can expect everyone to tell the truth. And if they did, you wouldn't need trained judges. What never ceases to surprise me is that you all get so upset when people do lie their heads off in court.'

'Because they've taken an oath to tell the truth, that's why!'

'They'd probably much sooner not take an oath. But they're not given any choice, so it always seems unreasonable to blame them more for lying on oath than not on oath.'

'The oath is meant to ensure that they *will* speak the truth.'

'But does it really have that effect? Someone is either going to speak the truth or he's not and I don't suppose your hallowed oath makes any difference at all.'

'What's gone wrong with your day to make you voice such unprincipled sentiments?' he asked with a small smile. The signs were too obvious. When Philippa was contentious, she was worried about something.

'Peter phoned this morning,' she said, with a slight catch in her voice.

43

Matthew Chaytor's expression became suddenly wooden. 'Yes,' he said, 'and what is it this time?'

'He wants to come home for a bit.'

'Does that mean he's in trouble again?' he asked bleakly.

'I think he just feels the pressures building up.' She let out a sigh. 'Shouldn't we be grateful that he still turns to us at times of need?'

'I sometimes wonder, but I suppose so,' he said in a resigned voice.

Peter Chaytor was now approaching his twenty-first birthday, not that the event was likely to be celebrated in any of the customary ways. He was their only child and until the age of sixteen had been an exemplary son, doing well at school both academically and in the field of sport. Then almost overnight he had changed. He ceased to work hard, or even work at all, and lost all interest in games. The climax came when he broke out of school one night and took a foreign au pair girl to a party in a disco in the neighbouring town which was strictly out of bounds. As a result of this escapade he had been expelled.

For the next year he sat around at home, ostensibly working for 'A' levels, but, in fact, spending most of the day in bed and going out each evening with dubious friends. Finally, he left home (without warning) and his parents heard nothing of him for just over a week. Then he phoned to say that he was all right, but wouldn't be coming back.

Since his initial departure, he had returned twice, on each occasion as a result of a scrape with the police. On the first he had been detained and questioned about some cannabis found at the address where he and five others lived in squalor. On the second he had been questioned about his possession of a silver snuff box after trying to sell it to a dealer, who had become suspicious and notified the police. In fact he had stolen it from his own home, but when the police officer telephoned Philippa, she told him that she had given it to her son to try and sell. Nobody really believed her, but it put an end to any question of criminal proceedings being launched.

When he learnt what his wife had done, Matthew Chaytor was secretly thankful that he had not been in her shoes when the police phoned. He rather believed that he would not have bailed his son out in the circumstances, but it would have been an agonising decision.

That had happened a year ago, shortly before he became a judge. Since then Peter phoned at irregular intervals usually at times when he was certain that his father would be out. Philippa always told her husband about the calls, without going into details. He, for his part, normally refrained from asking too pertinent questions.

'When's he coming?' he asked.

'He didn't say. In the next few days, I gathered.'

Matthew Chaytor raised his eyebrows. 'He usually comes running immediately when he needs us at all. Where was he calling from?'

'He didn't say, but he's been working for someone who owns a roadhouse. I think he said it was called the Monkes Tale.'

CHAPTER FOUR

'You could have knocked me down with a feather when someone mentioned the name of the judge,' Jakobson expostulated. 'Why didn't you tell me, Pete, that your dad was an Old Bailey judge?'

'I didn't know he was. I'd no idea where he did his judging,' Peter Chaytor replied, tugging nervously at the straggling ends of his beard.

'Well, thank goodness I didn't know when I was actually in the witness-box or I'd never have been able to go through with it. It was bad enough without that.'

Jeff Jakobson shook his head in apparent recollection of the ordeal. They were in his office at the Monkes Tale, the throbbing music of the disco lightly pummelling the door. Peter Chaytor was slumped in a chair, but Jakobson was standing on the edge of the raised brick hearth which jutted out into the room. It was a favourite pose and, with hands thrust deep into his trouser pockets, he rocked himself to and fro on the balls of his feet.

'He'd never heard of you, so there was no need to get het up.'

'I didn't get het up, but only because I didn't know it was him. I never would have known if the police officer hadn't said something about Judge Chaytor to the geezer who paid us our expenses. So as we were leaving, I asked him if he meant it was Judge Chaytor in our case and he said yes.'

Peter Chaytor said nothing. The trouble with Jeff Jakobson was that he would go on and on about something and he always had to dramatise every event in his life. So far as he, Peter Chaytor, was concerned, his father was as remote as the man in the moon and he was bored

47

by all this carry-on. Coincidences happened all the time, some more remarkable than others and he couldn't see anything so remarkable about this one. His own plight was of far more immediate interest.

Two days ago he had been stopped by the police for speeding. At the time he was driving Jeff Jakobson's new car, with his permission. The police had been suspicious and heavy-handed as they were apt to be with long-haired and scruffily dressed young men who crossed their path. While one of the officers had been laboriously recording both the car's and Peter Chaytor's particulars, the other had walked round to the back and opened the boot where he had found four cases of whisky.

After that the questions had come like machine-gun fire and the upshot had been that he had been forced to accompany them to a nearby police station. There, after further questioning, he had finally been allowed to go, but had been bailed to return in fourteen days' time when he would be told whether any criminal charge was going to be preferred against him in respect of the whisky, which the police clearly suspected as being stolen property.

'Have the police been in touch with you yet about the whisky?' he asked in an anxious voice.

Jakobson frowned. 'No, but what are you worried about, Pete? There was nothing funny about the whisky.'

'Except it was nicked.'

'Who says? I didn't nick it, you didn't nick it. The police can't prove a thing.'

'They can find out that it was part of a lorry load that went missing.'

'So? That doesn't prove I knew it had been stolen when I bought it.' I'll tell them I was offered a bargain and I took it.' A cunning look came into his eyes. 'But of course it wasn't such a bargain that a reasonable person like myself must have had his suspicions.' He gave Peter Chaytor a confident smile. 'And if the police can't touch

48

me, they certainly can't touch you, Pete. All you were doing was collecting the stuff on my behalf.'

'They can do me for speeding.'

'Who doesn't get done for speeding? Even judges and coppers themselves get taken to court for that.' He stretched out his arms and yawned noisily. 'I reckon that in a couple of years' time, I'll have made enough to get out and then it'll be the good life of sunny Spain for Jeff Jakobson. I've got my eye on a nice little property on the Costa del Sol. I'll have a boat and there's a golf course nearby and there'll be lots of cheap brandy . . .'

'You'll probably be bored stiff inside of a month.'

'Not your Jeff! I'll have things to do. It's having the right contacts in life that matters, Pete.' The remark was accompanied by a knowing wink. He glanced at his watch. 'I'm expecting a visitor shortly, Pete, so I'll see you tomorrow.'

'Will you be going back to the Old Bailey?'

'Not likely. Mind you, I'd like to be there when Tanner gives his evidence, just to hear what he says. Not that it'll be the truth!'

'What is the truth? Why did he take your car?'

'Not for a joy-ride, that's for sure.'

'Why then?'

'He was going to use it on a job.'

'How'd you know?'

Jakobson tapped the side of his nose with his forefinger. 'I keep my eyes and ears open. You have to in this business.'

'What job was he going to use it on?'

'Don't ask so many questions. It's not healthy to get too interested in things that don't concern you. That's my advice to you, Pete.'

Peter Chaytor gave a shrug of indifference and got up from his chair. Without another word, he turned and left the room.

Jakobson stared at the closing door with a frown. He had first met Peter Chaytor one Sunday evening two months previously at a friend's flat in Earls Court. There'd been a lot of aimless young people present and he had soon decided that it wasn't his scene. He had been about to leave when his host had pointed out Peter Chaytor, mentioning that his father was a judge. On an impulse, Jakobson had approached him and got into conversation, seeking to give the impression that he was the only person in the room who merited his attention. It had not been long before Chaytor had said he was on the vague look-out for casual work and Jeff Jakobson had not been able to resist playing the role of benefactor of the young. The outcome was that a few days later Chaytor turned up at the Monkes Tale and had been there ever since, though there had been times when Jakobson had regretted his quixotic offer. He was a strangely moody youth, with a temper lurking beneath his often torpid façade.

For the most part, he was Jakobson's personal factotum and he seldom came into contact with the customers. He occupied a small room over the kitchen at the back of the premises and remained generally aloof from the rest of the staff. Soon after he had arrived, he had asked Jakobson not to tell people that he was the son of a judge. He gave as reasons that he wasn't proud of the fact and that it was strictly a non-event. Irrelevant and without interest.

Jakobson glanced at his watch again. His visitor was late. But he had scarcely registered the fact before there was a peremptory knock on the door. There was no time to say 'come in' before Sweetman strode into the room.

'Good evening, Totty, have a chair and a drink and tell me what I can do for you?'

*　　　　*　　　　*

When T.D.C. Bramley arrived back at his station, he reported on the day's events to his detective inspector.

'Do I need to hear about a traffic case?' D.I. Shotter asked wearily. 'I've got enough proper crime on my plate to keep me busy till Christmas and beyond. You'd better go and tell Inspector Ansett. If anyone's interested, it'll be him.'

'I thought I'd better mention it to you, sir, as the case seems to have undertones.'

'What sort of undertones?' Shotter asked without enthusiasm.

'Curious features, sir . . .'

'Look, Pat, unless you're going to ask me to drop everything else and send me into immediate action, I'd sooner not know. If it's merely some hunch you've formed, play around with it yourself. I just haven't the time to listen. It wasn't a C.I.D. enquiry in the first place, so have a word with Inspector Ansett. He's the king of traffic.'

Patrick Bramley accepted his rejection and made his way to Inspector Ansett's office. He found the inspector putting on his overcoat in preparation of going out.

'Yes?' he said, warily.

'I just came to report on the Tanner trial at the Old Bailey, sir.'

'Convicted, was he?'

'It's not over yet.'

'But going all right? It was a bad case, I recall. Driving along a dark, narrow lane at a furious speed. And the victim was a friend, wasn't he?'

'I gather so, sir. The mystery is what they were both doing in Waterworks Lane at that hour of the evening?'

'You're not particular about your route when you're joy-riding. A turn here, a turn there, it's all part of the fun until you're caught.'

'But that doesn't account for the victim's presence in the lane.'

'As I recall the evidence, the inference was that he had stepped out to try and flag Tanner down.'

51

'It still leaves some loose ends around, sir.'

'Such as?'

'Why he should have been trying to flag down the car?'

'Great Scott, Bramley, we've got enough to do without trying to prove what we don't have to prove. In this case, you have evidence of a car being driven at a reckless speed which hits an unfortunate pedestrian and kills him. All very sad, but all very straightforward, so don't start looking for complications.'

'That's another thing, sir,' Patrick went on stubbornly, 'the only evidence of the manner in which the car was being driven comes from a right villain, Billy Cox.'

Inspector Ansett sighed and adjusted his peaked cap on his head. 'We have to take the evidence as we find it, Bramley. Even a villain can't be proof against witnessing a traffic accident. Mind you, I'm not saying Cox would have come forward if the officers hadn't happened to find him at the scene. In the circumstances, however, he didn't have much choice and there's never been any reason to doubt his evidence.

'Now I really have to be on my way. I've promised to take my wife to the cinema this evening.' He reached the door and opened it. Over his shoulder he said, 'Let me know the result of the case.'

The office which Patrick Bramley shared with two other detective constables and a detective sergeant was deserted when he reached it. As the most junior occupant, his own desk was a short, battered trestle table which had been pushed up against the wall in the farthest corner from the window. It was not that his colleagues had ostracised him, simply that an office meant for one now accommodated four.

At least he had his own telephone and a temperamental table lamp that someone had found buried under a pile of junk at the back of the cupboard.

As he walked over to his so-called desk, he reflected that

you had to be dedicated to work under such conditions. He didn't blame Inspector Ansett for wanting to hurry off to take his wife to the cinema, still less did he hold it against D.I. Shotter that he hadn't wished to hear what he had to tell him, even though the absence of encouragement could hardly have been more marked. The basic problems were too much crime for too few officers and diminished morale throughout whole seams of the C.I.D. structure as a result of a succession of scandals involving bribery and corruption.

He sat down and pulled the telephone toward him. Well, at least Jennie could be the beneficiary of his superiors' lack of interest. He was hers for the whole evening.

He dialled her number and wondered whether it would be she or her mother who answered. Her father worked in Scotland for a company concerned with North Sea oil development and came home only at weekends. Patrick hardly knew him, but he got on well with Mrs King.

'Hello, darling, it's me,' he said, recognising Jennie's voice on the line. 'What time shall I come and pick you up?'

'Oh, Pat, I can't come out this evening. Mum's not been well all day and she's in bed. She won't have the doctor, but she keeps on needing me.' Her voice carried a note of intense disappointment.

'Is there anything I can do? Shall I come round?'

'I don't think there's anything to be done. If she's not better in the morning, I'll send for the doctor, anyway. Come round about nine. With luck, she'll be asleep by then and I shan't be dashing up and down the stairs all the time. I think it's only one of these twenty-four-hour upsets – at least, that's what Mum says – but I can't leave her the way she is.'

'Of course you can't, darling.'

'But oh, Pat, isn't it rotten that the one evening you're free I'm not.'

'At least your mother's not normally as demanding as the police,' he said with a small laugh. 'See you about nine o'clock. Call me here if you need anything.'

'Are you going to stay at the station?'

'I might as well. I've got one or two things I can do and I'll nip along to the canteen later for a quick bite.'

After he had rung off, he unlocked one of the cupboards in which the C.I.D. files were kept. He found the ones he was looking for and returned to his desk.

If he was going to start probing, he had first to brief himself on the backgrounds of the leading participants.

Before the evening was through, he had fetched further files and made a number of telephone calls, including one to a friend who worked in the criminal intelligence branch at Scotland Yard.

He was about to go and rummage for another file when his phone rang.

'I thought you were coming round at nine,' Jennie said reproachfully.

'I am. What time is it now?'

'Half past!'

'Oh, lord! I'm terribly sorry, darling, I'll drop everything and come now.'

As he locked away the files and fled the office, he had a distinct feeling of satisfaction. It was as if he had blown the dust off the pieces of a puzzle. They still had to be correctly slotted together, but, at least, they were now identifiable.

No, he saw himself more like a picture restorer who starts to clean a picture only to discover that it has been painted on top of another.

He could still see only a traffic accident depicted on the canvas in front of him, but he now felt that a quite different picture lay beneath it.

CHAPTER FIVE

Matthew Chaytor spent a restless night, dozing and surfacing from disturbed dreams wondering what he ought to do.

Before going to bed he had checked in the telephone book and found that only one Monkes Tale was listed. It was as he had feared and he hadn't really expected to be let off the hook so easily.

It meant that Peter must be working for the slippery witness, Jakobson, who had yesterday cut such a poor figure in the box.

The fact that his son now worked for a man whose car had been stolen six months previously while its owner was on holiday was not significant on the face of it. It wouldn't normally give rise to any sinister implications. Nevertheless, he was left with a feeling of uneasiness which remained even after Philippa had said that, so far as she knew, Peter had not been at the Monkes Tale for more than a few weeks.

It was not a problem he could discuss with Philippa, if only because she wouldn't see it as one. She had never shown much understanding of the ethics governing his profession, dismissing them as so much cant and hypocrisy.

A large part of her bias sprang from the belief that, in a world of increasing equality between the sexes, the English Bar was male dominated and that for women barristers the struggle to survive was anything but equal. She could, when roused, become quite passionate on the subject of feminine rights.

He felt his dilemma the greater for being a new judge and for sitting at the Old Bailey for the first time in his judicial life. And what a factory it had become since the days he had practised there as a young man!

He did know one or two of the court's permanent judges and he decided that, if he arrived a bit early, he might go and seek the advice of one of them. On the other hand he might not. It would mean talking about Peter and he always found that painful.

Philippa was in the kitchen when he came downstairs. Her breakfast consisted of a cup of lemon tea and an apple. However, she had plugged in the electric toaster and coffee pot for his use. The coffee pot was already making sounds like a thermal spring.

'Do you want an egg, Matt?' she asked as he sat down in the alcove at one end of the kitchen.

'Yes, please.'

'Two?'

'Just one.'

'Incidentally, I've phoned Lorna and put her off.'

Lorna was Philippa's sister and had a husband called Douglas who was a stockbroker. They had been due to have dinner with the Chaytors that evening.

'What did you tell her?'

'Simply that Peter might be turning up and we weren't sure how we'd find him. She understood.'

'Are you going to stay in all day on the off chance that he'll phone and appear on the doorstep?'

She turned round from the cooker which had been occupying her attention and faced him.

'Matt, I must.' Her tone asked for understanding. 'I know you don't approve, but I'd never forgive myself if I felt I'd not been around when Peter needed me most. I could tell from his voice yesterday that he was steamed up about something and, knowing that, I must be on hand. There's nothing I can't rearrange. I'll phone Beryl at the shop and tell her that I shan't look in today.'

'I'd like you to call me at the Old Bailey if he turns up,' her husband said quietly.

She looked at him in surprise. 'What do you want to know?'

'First, I want to know how he is. After all, I am still his father. And secondly, I'd like to ask him about this place he's been working at, the Monkes Tale. I want to know if he's become involved in anything that might prejudice my continuing to act as judge in the case I'm trying.'

It was as he lopped off the top of his boiled egg that he realised he had dealt wth his problem in time-honoured fashion by postponing the moment of decision.

However, he still arrived at court on the early side. So did Ian Tanner; though by a different entrance.

*   *   *

When Gino Evans had eventually left Ian and Gail to go home the previous evening, it had been with the firm promise that he would devote the next day in trying to trace Mick Burleigh's sister. He had also hinted at making a cautious approach to Ron Hitching who, from what he'd heard, had been putting a bit of distance between himself and Totty Sweetman. Ian had urged him to put the rumour to the test.

The trouble was that Gino was idle and most of his promises went unfulfilled. But this time, with Gail in strong support of Ian's prodding, it seemed that he might be galvanised into action.

When Gail said this to Ian as they travelled to court the next morning, he remarked, 'I frightened him, that's the real reason. He's afraid I really will drag him into the shit with me.'

Gail hid her smile. It was no grief to her that Ian's friendship with Gino had deteriorated with the approach of his trial.

As soon as they arrived at the Old Bailey, he sought out the clerk from his solicitor's office. But no one had seen him and the presumption was that he hadn't yet arrived.

'What's he think he's meant to do for his money?' Tanner muttered indignantly. The fact that he was being defended at public expense had never been allowed to impinge on his mind. 'He's supposed to be looking after my interests, but he's about as much use as an empty beer bottle.'

It was at this moment that Tanner caught sight of Andrew Batchford and darted from Gail's side to waylay him.

'Can I have a word with you, Mr Batchford?'

Counsel halted in his tracks and turned round. 'Yes, all right. I'll be back in a couple of minutes. I just have to attend to another matter.'

When he returned, he joined Ian and Gail on the bench on which they were sitting.

'Is Mr Nicholson here?'

'Who's he?'

'Your solicitor's representative. However, perhaps we can get along without him. What is it you want to talk about?' He shot Gail a glance as though suddenly aware of her presence. 'Is this young lady with you?'

'She's my girl. She's giving evidence for me.'

'So you're Miss Norbet.'

Gail nodded and smiled nervously. Counsel gave her a small smile in return and looked back at Tanner.

'So what's on your mind?'

'It's about when I give my evidence. I want to tell a different story.'

'How different?' Andrew Batchford enquired in an ultra-cautious tone.

'It wasn't me that was driving the car.'

'Totally different, in fact,' Batchford observed in the

tone of one armoured against surprises by long experience of clients. After a short but heavy silence, he went on, 'I think there are one or two matters we must get straight, Mr Tanner. In the first place, the object of a trial is to elicit the truth and everyone who gives evidence, including the accused, is sworn to tell the truth.' Ignoring Tanner's sceptical look, he continued, 'Through your solicitors, you have provided me with a proof of your evidence and in that proof you admit to having been the driver of the car. We needn't canvass all the other details contained in your proof, it's the basic one which matters and which has been admitted by the defence.

'Now you tell me that you want to change your story. But the court is not concerned with stories so much as with truth. And the truth, Mr Tanner, is unchangeable.'

'It is the truth.'

'Since when?'

'What d'you mean?'

'If it's the truth, why is it only emerging now?'

'I was covering up for someone.'

Andrew Batchford sighed. 'Apart from any other considerations, let me give you this straight. If you go into the box and tell the jury that it wasn't, after all, you who was driving at the time of the accident . . . incidentally, were you in the car at all?' Tanner nodded. 'Because your fingerprints were found on the steering-wheel . . .'

'I can explain that.'

'Let me finish please. If you go into the witness-box and say you were not driving but were a passenger, the jury'll sink you without ever leaving court.'

'Why?'

'Why? Because it'll be obvious that you're lying. And if you're lying, the jury and the judge will take it as evidence that your driving was so dangerous and reckless that you didn't dare admit to being the driver. As I say, they won't believe you and they'll like you even less.'

59

'For telling the truth?' Tanner asked in a caustic tone.

'As I said just now, truth is unchangeable. It's not an adjustable commodity to suit one's convenience. Let me tell you something else. Prosecution witnesses are supposed to be cross-examined on the basis of a person's defence. I didn't ask Cox or Jakobson a single question suggesting that you weren't the driver of the car and weren't the person who took it from the car park. If you now testify that you weren't the driver, the judge is going to ask immediately why this wasn't put in cross-examination. What am I to tell him? That it wasn't your defence until this morning? Whatever way I dress up my answer, the judge is going to realise the truth and he'll tell the jury so when he comes to sum up.'

As he had listened, a look of obstinacy had come over Tanner's face.

'I could get off if the jury believed me,' he said determinedly.

'I'll go one better, you'd get off if they were left in a reasonable doubt as to whether you were the driver. But it's the "if" that's the sticking point.' He stared thoughtfully across the vestibule in which they were sitting and which had begun to resemble a mainline station at commuter time. When he refocused his attention, his look seemed to embrace Gail as much as Ian Tanner. 'I'd like you to think very carefully about what I've said. If you are determined to give evidence on the line you've indicated, because, as you now say, it's the truth, Mr Nicholson will have to take a fresh proof from you setting out all the details as fully as possible. Only then can we discuss the matter further and only then will I be able to tell you whether I can continue to defend you.'

'You mean you might ditch me?' Tanner asked aghast.

'What I mean, Mr Tanner, is that it might no longer be ethical for me to go on representing you. If you instruct me to put forward a defence which contradicts all you

60

have previously told me, I'd feel obliged to withdraw from the case. What it comes to is this. Before I can change course you must satisfy me that your new line really is the truth and in order to do that you must further satisfy me about your reasons for having withheld it until now.'

There was a tense pause and then Tanner asked, 'What do you think I'll get if I go down?'

'It depends what you're finally convicted of. In view of Jakobson's admissions under cross-examination, I hope the jury'll acquit you on the taking and driving away offence. I hope they'll decide that you had his permission to take the car, or, rather, that you thought you had. I think they should be ready to give you the benefit of the doubt, as the evidence stands at present.' He paused and added in a meaningful tone, 'Of course, they've yet to hear you in the witness box. As to the other charge, the causing death by reckless driving, I think the odds are you'll be convicted; but that if you stick to your existing defence there's a reasonable chance the judge will only impose a fine or, at worst, a suspended prison sentence. And, of course, you're bound to lose your licence for a few years. That's inevitable. He's a new judge and I've no idea how he views motoring offences, but I've no reason to think he's out of the ordinary. That's why I prophesy a fine or a suspended sentence.' Observing Tanner's expression, he went on, 'But if you give evidence denying you were the driver, but are nevertheless convicted, I think you'll stand a good chance of being put inside. After all, conviction in those circumstances would mean that the jury had rejected your defence and, in effect, would have decided that you'd committed blatant perjury. You'd have been found guilty of as bad a case of causing death by reckless driving as one could imagine, leaving your unfortunate victim to die in the road while you disappeared into the night. The proof that you were the driver is strong,

61

Mr Tanner. Whatever you may think of us lawyers, don't underestimate a jury's common sense!'

'That prosecuting counsel's not much good, is he?'

'Don't pin false hopes on his inadequacies!' He looked directly at Gail and said wearily, 'You've heard everything I've said, Miss Norbet. Make him see a bit of sense.'

'I've a good mind to give *him* the bleeding sack,' Tanner muttered mutinously as Andrew Batchford hurried off to counsel's robing room. 'He as good as said I was a liar. Christ! Why'd I have to be given a mouthpiece who gets all uptight over what's proper and not proper?' Gail gave his hand a placating squeeze. 'I still think it could be worked up into a decent defence. I wish now I'd thought of it sooner. Bloody Gino, why should he get away with it?'

Further recrimination was forestalled by someone calling out his name outside the entrance to the court. He gave Gail a quick peck on the cheek and got up to walk over and surrender to his bail.

'Good luck, Ian,' she said softly with a slight catch in her voice, as he left her side.

He noticed his counsel speaking to T.D.C. Bramley as he threaded his way across the court and frowned. What the hell did he have so much to talk to the police about? As far as Tanner was concerned, it was like fraternising with the enemy. However, the judge's entry soon put an end to the conversation.

After the usual exchange of bows between judge and counsel, with one to the jury thrown in, which Ian Tanner observed contemptuously, the trial got under way again.

The first witness of the day was Police Constable Leach who had been the driver of the panda car which had chased the Ford Granada.

He was a heftily built young man who looked ready to burst out of his uniform. In answer to Mr Ridge's questions he told the court that he had been driving the car on the evening in question, with P.C. Yardley as his co-driver, and had been about to turn left at a T junction with a green light in his favour when a Ford Granada car, registration number OYN 703R, had swerved across his bows coming from the right, narrowly missing the police car and accelerating away at a furious speed. He described how he had given chase, just managing to keep it in sight until it had turned off the main road with screeching tyres and had disappeared from view. Luckily, the witness knew the local geography and guessed that the car might have ducked down Waterworks Lane. This was confirmed when they saw the reflection of its lights about a quarter of a mile ahead. He explained that there was no lighting in Waterworks Lane and that was why they were able to pick out the car lights.

'What lights did it have on?' asked Mr Ridge in a tone of self-approbation.

'When it first turned into Waterworks Lane it was showing dipped headlights, sir, but these were soon switched off.'

'You were able to tell that, were you?'

'I was, sir.'

'Yes, kindly continue.'

'I should add, sir, that when we turned into Waterworks Lane, P.C. Yardley and I wound down our respective windows and were able to hear the engine noise of the car ahead.'

'What sort of noise was it, officer?'

'It was the noise of a car being driven at high speed, sir.'

'And what happened next?'

'We rounded a bend and I saw a man stooping down in the road and a body lying there. I stopped the car and we both got out. It was the witness Mr Cox. As a result of what he told us, I got back into the car, leaving P.C. Yardley at the scene, and drove along the lane, which peters out about three hundred yards further on. Just before that point, I saw wheel marks on the grass verge. I stopped and went to investigate and found the Ford Granada car abandoned in some trees about twenty-five yards off the road.' P.C. Leach paused and with the air of one delivering a *coup de grâce* added, 'There was no sign of the driver.'

Mr Ridge nodded magisterially and, wrapping his gown around him, sat down with a flourish.

Judge Chaytor blinked a couple of times and then said, 'Do you not wish to ask this witness whether he was able to see the driver's face at any stage?'

'Didn't I do that, my lord?'

'No, Mr Ridge, you didn't.'

'An oversight, my lord. Officer, you've heard what my lord has just said, did you have an opportunity of seeing the driver's face?'

'Yes, I did. It was the defendant, Tanner.'

'Oh, really!' Andrew Batchford had jumped to his feet in an outburst of forensic indignation. 'I must protest, my lord. A dock identification of that nature is most prejudicial in the circumstances. There's never been an identification parade and the prosecution know perfectly well that an identification sprung like that is most improper.'

'I don't think you can blame Mr Ridge,' the judge said in a faint tone of surprise, 'he didn't actually invite the witness to make an identification. It just came out.'

'It was something which should have been guarded against, my lord. It is most unfortunate, and, as I've said, most prejudicial to my client.'

Matthew Chaytor frowned in a puzzled way. 'I hadn't realised, Mr Batchford, that identification was an issue in the case. I had been under the impression that your client didn't dispute he was the driver of the car.'

Blast! thought Andrew Batchford, have I put myself

too far out on a limb? Is it too late to crawl safely back again?

'My lord, I was objecting to the impropriety of a dock identification in principle . . .'

'I'm not sure that you're entirely justified even so,' the judge said equably. 'I accept that there was no identification parade – I assume one wasn't considered necessary because of the fingerprint evidence – but I observe from the witness' statement which formed part of the evidence on committal for trial that he gave a description of the driver. In those circumstances, I'm not so sure about the validity of your objection, bearing in mind that the description he gives in his original statement could be said to fit your client.'

'It could also fit a great many other young men, my lord,' Andrew Batchford said vigorously.

The judge shrugged. 'You're not, I hope, suggesting that what has slipped out from the witness is so prejudicial that I ought to order a re-trial in front of a fresh jury?' He paused. 'Because, in my view, such a course would not be warranted. When the time comes, I will certainly deal with the point when I direct the jury, but, meanwhile, I suggest the matter be regarded as closed.'

I got more hooked than I intended, Andrew Batchford thought to himself, but the judge has let me off.

'I have no wish to pursue the matter further in view of your lordship's observations,' he said and sat down with a small bow.

Throughout the exchange, P.C. Leach had stood with a stolid expression. It was impossible to divine whether he had slipped in his identification of Tanner as a quick trick or out of genuine unawareness of the ever modified law on the subject. He looked neither surprised, disconcerted, nor yet satisfied at the forensic furore he had caused.

Meanwhile Mr Ridge had resumed his seat, grateful that

he had been able to keep his own head below the parapet during the skirmish. He had been feverishly trying to look up the latest cases on identification while Andrew Batchford and the judge slugged it out.

'You have no further questions to ask the witness, Mr Ridge?' Matthew Chaytor enquired, glancing down at the seated figure.

'No, my lord,' prosecuting counsel replied with unusual firmness.

'You doubtless wish to cross-examine, Mr Batchford?'

Andrew Batchford nodded and rose to his feet again, though not with the degree of eagerness the judge had expected.

'As I understand your evidence, officer, you never saw the car after it turned into Waterworks Lane until you found it abandoned, is that correct?'

'Yes, sir.'

'So you can give no estimate at all of the sort of speed at which it was being driven in Waterworks Lane, that's right, isn't it?'

'It was being driven very fast, sir.'

'How can you tell?'

'I could hear the engine noise ahead, sir.'

'That could have been because it was in a low gear. It wouldn't necessarily denote speed, would it?'

'It was definitely being driven at a fast speed, sir,' P.C. Leach repeated doggedly. Defending counsel will try to twist and turn every answer, but you mustn't give an inch, he had been told at training school.

Andrew Batchford sighed. It was like trying to argue with a gramophone record.

'You have also said that the car's dipped headlights were extinguished after the car had turned into Waterworks Lane.'

'Yes, sir.'

'That's pure guesswork on your part, isn't it?'

66

'No, sir.'

'How could you possibly tell?'

'Because I could see, sir.'

'What precisely could you see?'

'Suddenly there was hardly any light reflected at all.'

'That could have been because of the local topography, couldn't it?'

'Sir?'

'Because the car was moving behind a hedge or a high bank?'

P.C. Leach appeared to think. 'No, sir,' he said, after a pause.

'But Waterworks Lane does run between hedges and banks in places, does it not?'

'Yes, sir.'

'So how can you say that isn't the explanation?'

'I could tell, sir.'

Andrew Batchford glanced at the jury to discern their reaction to this somewhat unproductive dialogue, but their corporate expression was as impassive as that of the witness.

'You first saw the Ford Granada at the T junction?'

'Yes, sir.'

'You were about to make a left turn on a green light?'

'Yes, sir.'

'Did the light turn green as you arrived at the junction?'

'Sir?'

'Surely that's a simple enough question?'

'It turned green when we were about twenty-five yards distant from it.'

'Do you know what the timing of those lights is?'

'No, sir.'

'Do you know whether they were in correct working order that night?'

P.C. Leach frowned again, as though the possibility

of defective traffic lights had never come within his knowledge.

'I've no reason to think they weren't, sir.'

'Or any reason to think they were?'

'I've never known them out of order, sir.'

'So nobody's bothered to check?'

'If they hadn't been functioning properly, sir, someone would have reported the fact.'

'And because you know of no such report, you're swearing on oath that they were in order that night?'

P.C. Leach appeared to take a deep breath before answering. 'Yes, sir,' he said, as though making an unplanned crossing of the rubicon.

'Very well,' Andrew Batchford said in a tone designed to undermine further the witness' self-confidence.

T.D.C. Bramley, who had been keenly following the cross-examination, found himself admiring P.C. Leach's rocklike performance. It was all very well people criticising police officers for displaying stupid inflexibility when giving evidence. If they did concede a point, it took less than no time for defending counsel to start exploiting the gain and holding the witness up as hopelessly unreliable.

'I think you said the car shot across your bows and had to swerve to avoid hitting you?'

'Yes, sir.'

'And then it accelerated away, you said?'

'Yes, sir.'

'I suppose that part of the affair couldn't have occupied more than a few seconds?'

'No, sir.'

'And most of your attention would have been concentrated on avoiding a collision?'

'I had to brake and pull hard over to my near side, sir.'

'Exactly. And so it was only during those few seconds and when your attention was necessarily concentrated elsewhere, that you had any opportunity of seeing the driver's face?'

A light seemed to dawn in the witness' eyes. 'I still saw his face, sir.'

'But only fleetingly?'

'P.C. Yardley saw him better, sir.'

'Ah! Have you adopted what P.C. Yardley told you later?'

'Sir?'

'You're giving as your evidence what P.C. Yardley subsequently told you?'

'No, sir.'

'Was there anyone else in the car apart from the driver?'

'No, sir.'

'You mean, you didn't see anyone else?'

'Yes, sir.'

'But there could have been someone out of sight below the level of the windows?'

'I didn't see anyone, sir. Only the defendant.'

'Only the driver.'

'Yes, sir.'

The judge pulled fussily at his left eyebrow.

'Are you putting it to the witness, that your client was not the driver?' he asked in a puzzled voice.

'I am merely testing the witness' opportunity to have observed the various matters about which he has given evidence, my lord. No more, no less.'

Judge Chaytor seemed about to press his question, but then to have second thoughts. Instinct told him to move with circumspection. Andrew Batchford was a competent counsel and Matthew Chaytor sensed that he would be embarrassing him if he probed further. It would have been a different thing, had Mr Ridge been defending!

Shortly after this, Batchford sat down and Mr Ridge said that he would now call P.C. Yardley. By the time this witness had completed his evidence, which varied only marginally from that given by P.C. Leach, it was almost time to adjourn for lunch.

Announcing that he proposed to adjourn a few minutes early, Matthew Chaytor left the bench and retired to his room to telephone his wife.

'Any news of Peter?' he asked as soon as she answered.

'None.'

'Not even a phone call?'

'Not a word.'

Neither of them had any inclination to remark that no news was good news, knowing it not to be true.

'I'll call you again before I go back into court this afternoon.'

'All right. I'll be here, Matt.'

While the judge was making his phone call, T.D.C. Bramley and Andrew Batchford were talking in the now emptied court-room.

'Supposing for one moment that my client wasn't driving, who do you suppose might have been?'

'Is that what Tanner's now saying? That he wasn't driving?'

Andrew Batchford's expression remained straight-faced. 'My question was entirely hypothetical.'

Patrick Bramley smiled. 'Then the answer's wide open.'

'Meaning?'

'That it might have been anyone.'

'Not necessarily Evans? You don't think he'd cover up for him?'

'Why should he?'

'Because, as I understand it, Tanner, Evans and Burleigh were mates who hunted together.'

'Why should Evans ask or allow Tanner to take the rap for him?'

'Well, if it wasn't Evans, who was it?'

'As I've said, the answer to that is wide open. If Tanner wasn't the driver, it would mean that even more lies

70

beneath the surface than you've supposed, Mr Batchford.'

Defending counsel was thoughtful for several seconds. 'Anyway, you can't think of anyone else he might want to protect?'

'From what little I know of Tanner, I can't think of anyone at all. He doesn't sound the sort of person to take the blame for other people's mistakes, let alone their criminal acts.'

'I'd find it hard to disagree with that view,' Batchford remarked dryly. 'Anyway, thanks for your words of wisdom. I get the impression that we'd both stake our money on Tanner having been the driver, which answers my question. My *hypothetical* question, that is.'

'It's the non-hypothetical questions hanging around the case which are less easily answered.'

'Ah! I'm glad you think so. I can see you've come round to sharing my view that all is not as straightforward as it appears.' He gave Patrick a resigned look. 'Though whether the truth, should it ever emerge, would assist my client is entirely another matter. It's sometimes embarrassing to an advocate to know too much.'

CHAPTER SIX

Gino Evans felt far from sure that Ian Tanner wouldn't seek to shop him if and when he found himself finally cornered. He had been aware of the possibility for some while, but last night was the first time it had actually surfaced. Ian would be capable of dragging him in either to help himself or out of spite to ensure he didn't sink alone.

Gino had always avoided trouble when he could and it was this, more than anxiety about what Ian could actually do to him, that prompted him into action.

He knew that Ron Hitching was a packer with a firm of stationery wholesalers in Mitcham. He also knew that he invariably spent his lunch break between the pub opposite and the betting shop next to it.

He arrived in the area and parked his car in a side street near the pub. There was no sign of Hitching in any of the bars nor in the betting shop next door. Thus satisfied, Gino bought himself a pint of beer and settled himself in a corner of the public bar from where he could watch the comings and goings.

Just before one o'clock, Hitching came into the bar with an older man. They were dressed in identical dark blue overalls with the firm's monogram stitched on to a breast pocket, from which Gino inferred that the older man was a work-mate.

He watched them go up to the bar where Hitching ordered and paid for their drinks.

The older man pulled out a packet of cigarettes. Hitching accepted one and they lit up.

It seemed to Gino an age before Hitching cast a glance round the bar. It was not that they were in any deep conversation; indeed, their exchange of words was desultory in the extreme. But for all that Hitching's eyes seemed riveted to their small bit of counter with its two pints of beer.

Eventually, however, he shifted his position and in so doing let his gaze go round the bar.

Gino was ready and gave him a small nod of recognition. Hitching frowned slightly, but made no other response. A couple of minutes later, however, when the older man headed for the toilet, Hitching came across to where Gino was sitting. His expression was unfriendly and his tone, when he spoke, did nothing to belie it.

'What are you doing here?' he asked.

'I was hoping to be able to have a word with you, Ron,' Gino said, realising that it was not a time for pretence. Hitching wasn't ever going to believe that their meeting was fortuitous.

'What about?'

'Ian Tanner's up at the Old Bailey?'

'What's that got to do with me?'

'You used to know Mick Burleigh's sister.'

Hitching gave him a suspicious look. 'What of it?'

'Mick used to talk about you.'

'What are you trying to tell me?'

'Gather you don't see so much of Totty Sweetman these days.'

Hitching cast a quick, furtive glance round the bar, at which moment his colleague emerged from the toilet and returned to where they had been doing their drinking.

'I can't talk here,' Hitching said in a strained tone.

Gino nodded understandingly. 'What about when you've finished work, can we meet then?'

'Where?'

'What about the Monkes Tale?'

'I keep away from that place.' A thoughtful look came into his eyes. 'I don't mind meeting you in the car park.

My girl lives close to the Monkes Tale, so it'd be quite handy. We can talk in the car, it'll be better than some pub. More private. When I say we can talk, I mean you can talk. I'm not promising to say anything.'

'What time?'

'Nine o'clock. I'll park at the far end.'

'All right,' Gino said, with a faint note of hesitation.

'If you're not going to turn up, say so and save us all a bit of trouble.'

'Of course, I'm going to turn up.'

'I thought you sounded a mite doubtful.'

Gino shook his head energetically. 'No.'

'After all it's you who wants to talk to me, not the other way round,' Hitching remarked, fixing him with a quizzical stare.

'I know.'

'I'm the one who's doing the favour.'

'I appreciate it. Ian Tanner'll appreciate it.'

'O.K., then. Nine o'clock in the Monkes Tale car park.'

Hitching rejoined his companion at the bar and didn't give Gino so much as another look, not even when he passed close by him on his way out ten minutes later.

Gino, on the other hand, scarcely took his eyes off Hitching, as he tried to decide whether the other was out to trick him. He had achieved his object beyond expectation and now he was having second thoughts. Ron Hitching had agreed to meet him and Gino was wondering why. He thought backwards and forwards over their conversation and finally decided that his suspicions were unfounded. Though that didn't mean he wouldn't take a few precautions of his own before getting into Hitching's car that evening.

The truth was that he had expected an outright rebuff and not received one. Was he right to be suspicious or was Ron Hitching really ready to talk? Of course, he hadn't said he would, only that he'd listen. But why should he be ready to listen unless . . . Unless what? Unless he was also ready to talk. Moreover, what was he expecting to hear?

Gino drained his glass, picked up his lighter and packet of cigarettes which he had placed on the table and rose.

His step was almost jaunty as he walked out of the bar. Confidence had flooded back. He held the whip hand and Ron Hitching realised it, otherwise he would never have agreed to their meeting. Hitching's attitude also confirmed the rumour that he had split up with Totty Sweetman. A pity he hadn't heard that sooner. Anyway, he had achieved enough to keep Ian quiet for a bit longer.

All he had to do now was decide on his tactics for the evening.

*   *   *

Matthew Chaytor decided that he would prefer solitude to the company of the judges' dining-room. Accordingly, he asked to be brought some coffee and a sandwich, which he could eat in his room.

He also asked an usher to fetch his notebook from court.

While he ate, he read through the note he had taken of Jakobson's evidence. But, of course, it had not been his evidence so much as his demeanour which had condemned him. So far as the prosecution had been concerned, his evidence had been formal and uncontroversial. But then when Andrew Batchford had started to cross-examine him, Jakobson had watered down practically everything he had originally said. Matthew Chaytor didn't believe for a moment that Tanner ever thought he had the witness' unspoken approval of his taking the car and yet Jakobson had conceded this. It was very likely that the jury would acquit on the charge of taking and driving away the car without the owner's consent. Why had Jakobson decided to give him that let out?

The thought that Peter was associating with such an obviously devious individual was most disturbing.

76

Matthew Chaytor got up from his desk and went to sit in the room's only easy chair. It had to be at least partly his and Philippa's fault that Peter's life had veered off course. As a parent, he accepted that. He also accepted that, in any apportionment of blame, his was greater than Philippa's.

But that didn't assist in deciding where he, in particular, had gone wrong and what he could have done to have prevented it happening.

He had always thought he got on well enough with his son. But perhaps that was part of the trouble; he had played the conventional father without observing that he didn't have a conventional son. It was certainly true that he had seen less of him in his formative years than he would have wished, but that was the price exacted by hard-earned success at the Bar. Devotion to his profession had meant a certain neglect of family. Some avoided this pitfall and others had families where no harm was done anyway.

Was it possible now to bridge the gap that ever widened between him and Peter? If he was given the chance, he must try. But that belonged to the misty and uncertain future. The present was that he was due back in court in ten minutes time.

He reached out for the telephone and rested it on his lap as he dialled his home number.

Philippa must have been sitting beside it, for she answered immediately.

'Any news?' he asked.

'No, not a word.'

'I'll be back about five o'clock.'

'I'll be here.'

*   *   *

Peter Chaytor had spent the whole morning in his room over the kitchen. He had not spoken to Jakobson since

77

the previous evening, but had seen him go out and return about an hour later.

It wasn't long after he got back that a police car had driven into the car park. Two officers had got out, one in uniform the other in plain clothes, and entered the Monkes Tale.

Although visits by the police were not infrequent, most of them friendly and being quests for information, Peter felt certain that this one concerned himself.

He waited in his room, half-expecting to be summoned, but nothing happened. His anxieties had been partially allayed by Jakobson's display of confidence that there was nothing to get worried about. Nevertheless, the possibility remained that he wouldn't be able to talk himself out of this particular spot of bother.

Peter still remembered with horror the claustrophobic hours he had spent in a police cell when he had been detained in connection with a possible drugs offence. It wasn't any feeling of shame or degradation, just an animal's fear of the cage. He knew that if he were ever sent to prison, he would kill himself within the first twenty-four hours.

About forty minutes after they had arrived, the two officers emerged from a side door and walked across to their car, escorted by Jeff Jakobson, who appeared to be doing all the talking, accompanied by the usual amount of gesticulation.

The uniformed officer immediately got into the driver's seat, but the other stood for a moment beside the passenger's door as he listened to Jakobson.

Eventually he, too, got in and the car drove off. Jakobson looked preoccupied as he walked back to the building and disappeared from Peter Chaytor's view.

After waiting a further twenty minutes, Peter could bear the strain no longer and made his way down to

Jakobson's office.

He knocked on the door and opened it at the same time. Jakobson was in his favourite position, balanced on the edge of the brick hearth, hands thrust deep into trouser pockets, one of them rattling his small change.

'Oh, it's you!' he remarked sourly as Peter entered.

'I saw the police here. Was it about the whisky?'

'Too true, my friend! I don't mind telling you it was a very tricky interview.' He paused before adding vehemently, 'Thanks to your stupidity.'

'What did I do wrong?' Peter asked in a nettled tone.

'In the first place, it wasn't very clever to get stopped for speeding on a lark of that nature,' Jakobson remarked in a sarcastic drawl. 'A bit tactless to say the least, Pete.'

'It was unfortunate.'

'Bloody unfortunate! But that wasn't your only bit of silliness, Pete boy,' he went on in the same tone. 'For a judge's son, you're really not all that bright, are you?'

Peter Chaytor bit his lip. He had never taken kindly to any form of reproof and coming from this phony, dodgy, hail-well-met fellow, it was even less acceptable.

'Stop hectoring and tell me what the trouble is,' he said with an edge to his tone.

'Stop hectoring, indeed! You've a nerve. It's a pity you weren't hectored a bit more when you were a kid, then you might be something less of a liability now. O.K., I'll tell you what the trouble is. You left the flaming labels on.'

'Labels on the bottles you mean?' Peter said with a puzzled expression.

'Not on the bottles, idiot boy! On the cartons.'

'I didn't notice any.'

'Didn't notice any! I particularly told you to make sure all identifying labels were removed before you brought the stuff back.'

'I don't ever recall you saying that.'

79

'Of course, I did.'

'I don't think so.'

'Are you calling me a liar?'

'You're calling me one.'

'You're just a bloody idiot, you haven't got the brains to lie,' Jakobson shouted angrily.

'Don't shout at me, I don't like it . . .'

'I'll shout at you all I want.'

'Don't . . .'

'Go on, get out!' Jakobson's voice had risen to a bellow. Peter Chaytor hesitated, but Jakobson waved him imperiously to the door. 'Get out of my sight! We'll talk when I've calmed down a bit.'

'This afternoon?'

'When I send for you. Meanwhile, you'd better do some hard thinking. If I'm in a mess, so are you. And don't think you can get away with anything by saying you were only acting under my instructions, because I'll make sure that doesn't wash. And you'd better stop glaring at me if you want me to help you. Now, get!'

*   *   *

Just before Judge Chaytor returned to court at two o'clock, Andrew Batchford hurried down the dock steps to speak to his client who, in accordance with normal custom, was kept in custody during the lunch adjournment. It was only an hour's break and there was always a danger that defendants might be tempted to prolong it or to imbibe unwisely to forget the morning's ordeal and face the afternoon's. Hence the practice to keep even those who were otherwise on bail in custody while everyone else fought their way in and out of the building or into its cafeterias.

'Have you thought over what I said this morning?' Batchford asked.

'That bloody policeman couldn't have seen my face. He was too busy trying to avoid an accident.'

'At least we prevented the second one making a dock identification.'

'It's all loaded against one, i'n't it? The police can get away with anything.'

'That's not so, but we haven't time to argue about it. Can I take it that you will give evidence in accordance with your existing proof?'

'When'll I be giving evidence?'

'The prosecution will probably finish their case in the course of the afternoon and then you'll be in the box. That's why I had to speak to you now before the court sits.'

'I suppose I've got to, haven't I?' Tanner said morosely, after a considerable pause.

'Got to what?'

'Give evidence the way you want.'

'Don't try and lay any burdens on me. All I wish to know is what *you* have decided.'

'I haven't got much choice. All right, I'll stick to what I've already said.'

'I think you're wise,' Andrew Batchford said, without adding that he had been ready to bow out of the case if Tanner's decision had been otherwise.

The first witness of the afternoon was a uniformed sergeant named Griffin. He described how he had traced the ownership of the Ford Granada and how various enquiries at the Monkes Tale had led him two days after the event to interview Ian Tanner.

Evidence of Tanner's fingerprints on the steering-wheel had already been given by an officer who had made the necessary comparisons and Andrew Batchford was anxious that Sergeant Griffin shouldn't testify that he was already in possession of this evidence when he went to see Tanner, as it would indicate that his fingerprints were already on

81

file. Namely that he had a criminal record. Batchford had drawn prosecuting counsel's attention to the lurking danger and had then held his breath for fear that Mr Ridge might still blunder into it.

However, the moment of danger came and went as Sergeant Griffin described finding Tanner at his girl-friend's flat and taking him to the police station for inter-view.

'Had the defendant at this point admitted to you that he was the driver of the car?' the judge enquired, shooting defending counsel a quick glance.

'By implication, my lord.'

'What exactly do you mean by that?'

'I'd told him I had reason to believe that he was the driver and he hadn't denied it.'

'He never suggested you were mistaken about that?'

'Certainly not, my lord.'

'Yes, go on with your evidence, Sergeant Griffin. What happened at the station?'

'I put the allegations to him and cautioned him and he said he didn't wish to say anything at that stage. He was detained overnight and appeared in the magistrates' court the next morning when he was remanded on bail.'

'So he never gave you any explanation of what had happened?' Mr Ridge said in a tone of outrage.

'Not a word, my lord.'

Mr Ridge glanced meaningfully at the jury and sat down.

'Let's just clear this up in view of my learned friend's appearance of shock,' Andrew Batchford said amiably as he rose to his feet. 'The defendant didn't have to give you any explanation, did he?'

'It was a matter for him, sir.'

'Exactly. By that time you had cautioned him twice, once at the flat and again at the station?'

'Yes, sir.'

82

'And does the caution not contain the words, you are not obliged to say anything unless you wish to do so?'

'It does, sir.'

'And the defendant chose not to.'

'He did, sir.'

'So there's no occasion for shock or surprise, is there?'

'I've never said I was shocked or surprised, sir.'

'I accept that, sergeant,' Andrew Batchford remarked with an apologetic smile. 'It was my learned friend who appeared to be and I just wanted to put the situation into perspective for the jury.' .

'Which you seem to have done with a certain amount of guile, Mr Batchford,' the judge remarked.

'Thank you, my lord.'

'My observation wasn't exactly intended as a commendation,' Matthew Chaytor added firmly.

'What was the defendant's attitude when you first saw him at the flat?' counsel went on.

'He seemed very nervous.'

'Shocked, would you say?'

'Not what I'd call shocked, sir.'

'In what way did he show nervousness then?'

'He was all jumpy. He kept on fidgeting. He seemed to find it difficult to concentrate.'

'Wouldn't you agree that the last is an indication of shock?'

'I suppose it can be, sir.'

'Did it occur to you that he didn't wish to say anything because his recollection of events was still extremely hazy?'

'He never said so.'

'Was Miss Norbet present in the flat?'

'No, sir.'

'So you never saw her?'

'Only later when she came to the station.'

'Did she tell you that the defendant had been in a state of shock since the accident?'

'She said something to that effect, sir.'

'Thank you, Sergeant,' defending counsel said briskly and sat down.

At this point, there was agitated movement in the jury box and the foreman stood up to say that one of the jurors was feeling unwell.

Assisted by the jury bailiff, the juror in question left the court unsteadily and Judge Chaytor announced that he would adjourn proceedings for fifteen minutes.

Had it not been for this incident, Patrick Bramley would not have turned his head and looked up at the public gallery.

Seated at the rear and seemingly trying to merge into the background was Totty Sweetman.

Now what, he wondered, had brought *him* to court this afternoon? He was sure he had not been there in the morning.

There seemed to be one obvious answer. He had come along in the expectation of hearing Tanner give evidence. But why?

CHAPTER SEVEN

About half an hour later, the trial got under way again, the ailing juror having sufficiently recovered to resume his place.

'Don't suppose he was ill at all,' Andrew Batchford murmured to Patrick Bramley. 'Probably nothing worse than good old diarrhoea! I expect five minutes saw him all right again, but he couldn't come bouncing back too quickly after the bother he'd caused.'

With the judge back in his seat, Mr Ridge announced that the case for the prosecution was closed.

Andrew Batchford immediately called Tanner into the witness box, where he stood glowering until the usher handed him the Testament and a card bearing the words of the oath.

'Hold the Testament in your right hand and read out the words on the card,' the usher intoned.

'I swear by God the almighty . . .'

'By almighty God, start again, will you?'

He got through it at the second attempt and handed back the Bible and card with a furious look.

If he goes on wearing that expression, thought Andrew Batchford, the jury will think him capable of deliberately mowing down old ladies and children in their pushchairs.

'Is your name Ian Tanner?'

'Yeh.'

'How old are you?'

'Nineteen.'

'Do you have an occupation?'

'I've done different things. Do you want me to say what?'

'I think the jury might like to know.'

'I've been a van driver, I've worked in a newsagent's shop, I've done demolition work . . . Want me to go on?'

'No, you've given the court an idea. Just tell me this, did you have a job at the time of this accident?'

'No. I'd been doing odd jobs for friends.'

'We've heard that you used to frequent the Monkes Tale, in particular the Knightes Bar, is that correct?'

'Yeh.'

'And you knew Mr Jakobson?'

'Yeh.'

'On what sort of terms were you with him?'

'Fine.'

'You liked him?'

'Yeh.'

'And did he seem to like you?'

'S'right.'

'In what way would he show his liking?'

'He'd give me drinks. He also lent me money when I was skint.'

'Had you ever been out in his car?'

'Yeh.'

'With him?'

'S'right.'

'Had you ever driven it?'

'No. But I knew how to. And he often said he'd let me drive it.'

'I don't think that was put to Mr Jakobson, was it?' the judge asked peering at defending counsel.

'Perhaps not in specific terms, my lord,' Andrew Batchford replied, having been unaware that Tanner was going to add this embellishment.

'Are you sure that Mr Jakobson said that he would let you drive his car?' the judge asked, now turning to Tanner.

86

'Yeh, he did,' Tanner replied in a nonchalant tone.

'Very well. Yes, go on, Mr Batchford.'

'Coming to the night of September the second last, did you go to the Monkes Tale that evening?'

'Yeh.'

'About what time?'

'Half past eight.'

'Did you meet anyone there?'

'My mate, Gino.'

'Gino who?' the judge broke in.

'Gino Evans. Mick Burleigh was meant to meet us, but he never turned up, so there was just Gino and me.'

'What did you do?'

'We had a few drinks.'

'Then?'

'We decided to go outside for a bit of air. We also thought we'd look around for Mick.'

'Yes?'

'We were walking through the car park and there was Jeff's car.'

'That's Mr Jacobson?'

'S'right.'

'Did you know he was away in Spain?'

'Yeh, he'd told us he was going.'

'What happened next?'

'We thought we might have a bit of a ride.'

'In what?' Andrew Batchford prompted.

'In Jeff's car.'

'You say *we* thought. Who actually suggested it?'

'We sort of thought of it together, because we knew Jeff wouldn't mind.'

'And what then?'

'We tossed a coin to see who'd have first go and I won.'

'Yes?'

'And so I drove off just for a bit of a ride, because I knew Jeff had said he'd let me drive it.'

'Had he said the same thing to Gino Evans?' the judge enquired pointedly.

'Yeh, he must have done.'

'Why *must*?'

Tanner looked at Judge Chaytor as if sizing up a persistent mosquito. 'Otherwise Gino wouldn't have thought of driving it.'

Andrew Batchford, who felt irked at having his examination-in-chief interrupted by the judge's all too pertinent questions, decided that he must try to forestall further intervention by refusing to provide a pause between Tanner's answers and his next question.

'Was the car locked?' he asked, before the judge could follow up the somewhat ambivalent answer he had received to his own question.

'Yeh, but I happened to have a key that opened it.'

'How did you happen to have such a key?' he went on hurriedly, as he saw the judge about to interject his own question.

'I'd been working for a friend who runs a garage and I'd got a whole bunch of car keys.'

Andrew Batchford hoped it sounded more persuasive to the jury than it did to himself – or to Judge Chaytor from his expression.

'Were you still working for him at that date?' the judge enquired, before defending counsel could draw breath.

Tanner hesitated a fateful second. 'I must have been or I wouldn't have had the keys,' he said, as though that put an end to the matter.

'It doesn't necessarily follow,' the judge remarked glancing at the jury for tacit support.

'May I continue, my lord?' Andrew Batchford asked wearily in the silence that followed.

'Yes, Mr Batchford, I'm sorry if I've interrupted you, but I just wanted to get the position clear for the jury.'

'So you used the keys you happened to have with you to open the car?'

'Yeh.'

'And you drove out of the car park?'

'S'right.'

'Where was Gino?'

'I didn't see.'

'At all events, he wasn't in the car with you?'

'No.'

'Where did you drive?'

'I thought I'd just go for a quick turn and come back.'

'So which way did you go?'

'I crossed over the main road and went past some shops, then I took a left fork and drove along Bibby Road. There were some lights ahead of me, so I accelerated to get across while they were still green.'

'What were they showing when you reached them?'

'They were just changing to amber as I reached them.'

'Are you sure of that?'

'Yeh.'

'They weren't red?'

'No. I wouldn't have gone across if they'd been red.'

'What happened next?'

'This police panda car came shooting out of the street on my left and I had to swerve to avoid it.'

'And then?'

'It began to give chase. Flashed its lights and all that.'

'And what was your reaction?'

'I accelerated.'

'Why?'

'Because I realised it'd be a bit tricky to explain how I came to be driving the car. I mean, Jeff Jakobson was abroad and even though I knew he wouldn't mind my taking it, he wasn't around to say so. I thought it'd be best to avoid that bit of trouble.'

'That's why you tried to get away?'

'Yeh. It was sort of immediate reaction. Reflex, don't you call it?'

'Which way did you go?'

'I twisted and turned a bit and then I realised I was near Waterworks Lane and I thought I'd drive down there and leave the car at the end. I reckoned I could come back later and pick it up and return it to the car park.'

'But it didn't work out that way?'

Tanner hung his head for a second. 'No,' he said in a hoarse whisper, 'it didn't. I killed poor old Mick.'

'You say you *killed* him,' Andrew Batchford said, leaping in to try and add a gloss to this unhappy phrase.

'I don't mean I killed him on purpose. Mick was my mate. I just mean that I was driving the car which hit him.' A look of genuine anguish seemed to come over his face. 'I couldn't avoid him. He shot straight in front of the car as I came round the bend.' In a barely audible voice, he added, 'I didn't know it was Mick then. All I knew was that this figure had come out of the hedge on my left. It all happened in a flash. It was horrible.' He turned and looked at the jury with a beseeching expression. 'I swear I had no chance of avoiding him.'

Death-bed repentance, genuine contrition or a flare for theatricals? Andrew Batchford wondered which, as he paused to allow the jury time to be affected.

'What lights was the car showing at this time?' he asked in a suitably churchlike tone.

'I'd been driving on dipped headlights all the time.'

'P.C. Leach suggested in evidence that you switched them off after turning into Waterworks Lane and Mr Cox said that you only had on parking lights. What do you say to that?'

'They're both wrong. It would have been mad to have driven without the headlights on. There's no light in the lane and one couldn't have seen without headlights.'

From the moment he knew that his victim was Mick

Burleigh, Tanner had decided to say this. It played a part in easing his conscience. By the time the trial was reached, he had virtually persuaded himself that it was true.

'You say that the car hit Burleigh as you came round a bend, was it a right- or a left-hand bend?'

'Right hand.'

'And Burleigh came from your left?'

'Yeh.'

'So that your attention would have been focussed the other way, namely the way you were turning?' Andrew Batchford asked, deciding to slip the question through in leading form before anyone could object, not that Mr Ridge was likely to anyway. He was so busy covering the pages of his notebook with writing, it was doubtful whether his mind had time to consider what he was actually putting down. He reminded Batchford of a schoolboy frantically trying to keep up with a piece of dictation.

'S'right.'

'How far were you from him when, as you say, he shot out from the side?'

Tanner shook his head. 'Like I say, it all happened at once.'

'And as we've heard, it was the front nearside of the car that struck him?'

'That proves it, dun'it?'

'How fast were you going?'

'You can't drive fast in the lane. It's too narrow and twisty.'

'So how fast?'

'Not more than twenty-five.'

'Even though you were being chased?'

'I'd thought I'd thrown them off by then.'

'Now we know you didn't stop. Why not?'

'I was so shocked, I didn't know what I was doing. I just drove on in a sort of daze. Then I reached the end of the lane and left the car in some trees and staggered

91

away. I got to my girl-friend's flat, but I don't remember anything about it.'

'How long did you remain in this state of shock?'

'Several days.'

'Have you any idea what Burleigh was doing in Waterworks Lane that night?'

'No, it's all a complete mystery. He was meant to have met me and Gino at the Monkes Tale.'

'It sounds as if he was trying to waylay you in Waterworks Lane, do you think?'

'I know, but I can't explain it. I wish I could.'

'How would he have known you'd be driving along that particular route?' Judge Chaytor enquired, fixing Tanner with a penetrating look.

Tanner bit nervously at his lower lip. 'It's all a mystery.'

'Because,' the judge went on, 'as I understand your evidence, you took the car on the spur of the moment and thereafter didn't even decide to drive down Waterworks Lane until you reached it. That's right, isn't it?'

'S'right.'

'So how could Burleigh have known that the approaching car was being driven by you?'

Tanner gave a helpless shrug. 'I keep on telling you, it's all a mystery.'

'It is indeed!' the judge observed drily.

'When had you last seen Burleigh?' Andrew Batchford asked, realising that he now had a further hole to fill in.

'The previous evening.'

'At the Monkes Tale?'

'Yes.'

'And the arrangement was to meet there again the next evening?'

'Yeh. We used to go there once or twice a week. Sometimes more.'

'Had there been any talk with Burleigh about taking Mr Jakobson's car for a joy-ride?'

Oh God, I oughtn't to have asked him that, Andrew Batchford thought anxiously as he watched Tanner's expression. That was the trouble with clients like him, it was always risky to stray from the actual words of their proof.

' 'Course not,' Tanner said vehemently.

So, Burleigh *was* in on it, Patrick Bramley decided. The three of them had plotted to take Jakobson's car, but, for some reason, had deferred action until the following evening. Why? And why had Burleigh failed to turn up? And, most of all, how had he known the car would be driven along Waterworks Lane? And as to that, why drive along Waterworks Lane, anyway?

The questions succeeded each other like hurdles confronting an athlete.

It was at this point the judge chose to adjourn for the day.

CHAPTER EIGHT

Gino Evans arrived at the Monkes Tale early and parked his car close to the back of the building, a sprawling mock tudor affair with a turreted Gothic excrescence which was the Canterbury Grill Room. His car was a ten-year-old popular model that bore more scars than an unsuccessful prize-fighter. Its most recent conflict had been with a concrete pillar into which Gino had reversed violently, with the result that the passenger door had to be secured by wire and the boot could no longer be locked and had been given a cleft appearance.

He walked round the car park, but could see no sign of Ron Hitching sitting in his car. He decided to go and have a look around inside when he observed someone standing beside his car. As he approached, the person turned and Gino's heart skipped a beat as he recognised Totty Sweetman.

'Thought it was your car,' Sweetman remarked. He gave the offside wing a vicious kick and bits of dirt and rusty metal spattered on to the ground. 'Just seeing whether it'd pass its M.O.T. test.'

Gino laughed nervously.

'Haven't seen you around for some time,' Sweetman went on, turning his back on the car and facing Gino.

'I've not been here so often recently.'

'Not since Tanner's spot of trouble, eh?'

'No.'

Sweetman laughed, but there was nothing friendly in the sound. 'I hear he's up at the Old Bailey now. Drivers like him aren't safe to be on the roads. And nicking poor old Jeff Jakobson's car, too.'

Gino decided that silence was his wisest course. Totty Sweetman wasn't the sort of man you got funny with, particularly when he was only a yard from you.

'So what's brought you here this evening?' Sweetman asked, coming a step closer.

Gino swallowed hard. 'Just thought I'd look in.'

'Happened to be passing, eh?' Sweetman observed with a mirthless laugh.

'Yeah, that's right. Thought I might see one or two old familiar faces.'

'And you have, haven't you?'

'Yeah, yours, Totty!' Gino squeezed out a laugh.

'Not meeting anyone particular, then?'

'No.'

'Just wondered, when I saw you walking round the car park just now. Thought you might be looking for someone.'

'No. I'm going in, Totty, it's cold out here.'

Totty Sweetman grinned. 'Don't want to catch cold, do you? Nasty things, colds. Complications can set in, too.'

Gino grinned back as unconcernedly as he could. It was certainly true that he was shivering, though the temperature had little to do with it.

Leaving Sweetman, he dived through a side door and went along a short passage past Jakobson's office, then through another door at the farther end which opened into the main lobby. At the far side was an entrance into the Knightes Bar, which could also be reached direct from outside by another door. Gino couldn't see anyone he knew in the Knightes Bar and in any event his main concern was to get out the other side and creep back into the car park round the back of the premises.

Bumping into Totty Sweetman had shaken him and he had to find out whether his presence was fortuitous or whether he, Gino Evans, was about to be set up. If the latter, it could only mean that Ron Hitching was leading him by the nose.

He was about to leave the Knightes Bar by the outside door when Jakobson walked in. He stopped in his tracks and gave Gino a baleful stare.

'What the hell are you doing here?' he asked.

What Gino was prepared to take from Totty Sweetman was very different from what he'd take from Jeff Jakobson.

'That's no way to speak to a valued customer,' he said with a sneer.

'I told you to take your custom elsewhere.'

'So what! I go where I please.'

'Not here you don't! Now get off my premises and stay off or . . .'

'Or what?'

'I'll have you thrown out.'

'I'd like to see you try,' Gino retorted, pretending to shape up for a fight. 'You'd find yourself measuring the floor before you knew what had happened.'

Jakobson glared furiously and, giving Gino a sharp push, thrust past him.

As he made his way off the premises and was feeling calmer again, Gino decided he would seek out Jakobson after he had completed his business with Ron Hitching. He didn't really want to make an enemy of him. Jakobson had undoubtedly been in an unusually bad temper, but Gino also recognised that his own reaction had to a large extent been the overflow of his suppressed feeling toward Sweetman.

Moving cautiously and keeping within the shadow of the yard wall, he crept round the back of the Monkes Tale until he reached the corner of the car park. From here he was able to see where his own car was parked, but there was no sign of Totty Sweetman. He thought he could make out someone standing in the shadows beyond his car, but then decided it was an illusion caused by a shaft of light from an upper window of the building.

He skirted round the rear wall of the car park. A number of cars had arrived while he had been inside, but he was unable to see one resembling Ron Hitching's.

He had reached the far end and was moving stealthily toward the perimeter wall's junction with the road when he heard a faint 'psst'. He paused and peered ahead.

'It's me,' Hitching said in an urgent whisper. 'Come on. Quick.'

Gino emerged on to the pavement and could see Hitching standing beside his car about twenty yards along the road. By the time he got there, Hitching was in the driving seat and had started the engine.

'Get in, quick,' he said, as Gino came up to the car. Gino was no sooner inside than Hitching accelerated away from the kerb. 'I saw Totty's car there,' he explained. 'The last thing I'd want would be for him to see us together or he'd have got suspicious.'

Gino decided it was probably better not to mention his own encounter with Totty Sweetman as this might have added to Hitching's jumpiness.

They drove about a mile in silence. Then Hitching turned into a quiet side road, switched off the engine and lights and, turning to face Gino, said, 'Now, start talking.'

*   *   *

Tipped off by Sweetman to keep observation, Billy Cox had no difficulty in following Ron Hitching's car when it drove off with Gino in the passenger seat.

He saw the side road in which it parked, waited a few minutes, then drove slowly past it. A hundred yards on he turned his car round and drove back, bringing it to a halt in front of Hitching's so that the two cars were almost bonnet to bonnet.

At that moment he switched on his full headlights.

The reaction of the couple in the other car was dramatic. They ducked their heads as though expecting a hail of bullets.

'That'll do for starters,' Billy Cox murmured to himself as he pulled out sharply from the kerb and accelerated away.

A few minutes later, he was back at the Monkes Tale reporting to Totty Sweetman, who gave a satisfied nod.

'Now, let's go and find Jakobson,' Sweetman said, draining his glass of rum and peppermint.

*　　　　*　　　　*

It was half past ten before Gino arrived at Gail's flat where she and Tanner were waiting for him.

'Been expecting you for the past hour and a half,' Tanner remarked edgily. 'What the hell have you been up to? You were supposed to be meeting him at eight, weren't you?'

'Are you all right, Gino?' Gail broke in. 'Can't you see he's not well, Ian? Quick, he's going to fall.'

They both sprang toward him as he began to pitch forward and managed to get him on to the settee.

'Get me a drink,' Gino muttered, shaking his head painfully.

Gail fetched him some brandy which he took from her and gulped down.

'Another,' he said, holding out his glass.

Meanwhile, Tanner stood over him with a frowning, worried, and also slightly suspicious expression. 'What the hell's happened to you?' he asked, when Gino had taken a further gulp of brandy.

Though still shaken by his recent experience, Gino told them in faltering words of his meeting with Ron Hitching and how they had parked in a quiet street a mile or so away from the Monkes Tale after Hitching had spotted Sweetman's car. He told them too of his own encounter with Totty Sweetman in the car park.

Afterwards Hitching had been so unnerved that he refused to drive Gino all the way back to the Monkes Tale and had decanted him in the main road, leaving him over half a mile to walk.

'How far had you got with Hitching before Cox turned up?' Tanner asked in a voice that made it clear he was more interested in his own predicament than Gino's.

'I'd only just begun to chat him up.'

'Had you got anything out of him?'

'No, but I've a feeling he would have said something interesting.'

'Fat lot of good that is!' Tanner remarked bleakly. 'Means you'll have to work on him again.'

'Not much hope of that!'

'Don't talk like that! You've got to.'

'Use your nut, Ian! Ron Hitching's not going to be seen within a hundred miles of me. Also, I'd think he'll probably disappear for a while.'

'What, just quit his job?'

'What's a job compared with a body all in one piece. He was scared by what happened and I don't blame him.'

'It seems to me you're scared, too,' Tanner said in an unpleasant tone. 'Well, you'll have to find Tricia Burleigh.'

'You say that as if it was like going out and buying a packet of fags,' Gino retorted in an exasperated tone. 'It could take me ages to track her down.'

'It'd better not.'

Gail, who had listened in silence to what seemed to have become an almost nightly bicker, said, 'I'm still in the dark as to what you actually expected to find out from Hitching?'

Gino shot a sidelong glance at Tanner whose familiar frown once more took possession of his face. But neither of them spoke.

100

'Well, are you going to tell me, Ian?' Gail went on, with a note of stubbornness. 'What was Gino supposed to find out?'

With both Gino and Gail looking at him, Ian Tanner stared at the floor, his mouth turned down at the corners in a disgruntled expression.

'We wanted to know whether Sweetman's crowd knew anything about our taking Jakobson's car, that's all.'

'*Your* taking it,' Gino said quickly, moving along the settee as though to put distance between himself and any suggestion of guilt.

'That's not fair, Gino,' Gail said, turning on him. 'If the coin had come down the other way, you'd have been driving it. You were both in it together, it just happens that Ian got involved in something neither of you foresaw, but it's not fair to try and make out that you had nothing to do with the idea of taking Jakobson's car.'

'All right, all right!' Gino said, holding up his hands in mock surrender. 'I'm sorry if I said anything to upset anyone. Though if I had been the driver, there probably wouldn't have been an accident and then we'd all have been saved a lot of aggro.'

'Why wouldn't there have been an accident if you'd been driving?' Tanner asked abrasively.

Gino gave a resigned shrug. 'Because I reckon to be a better driver than you, Ian, that's why.'

'Balls to that! No one, not even the finest driver in the world, could have avoided hitting Mick.'

'We only have your word for that.'

'Do you want a bloody good punch on the head?'

'Can't you two stop quarrelling?' Gail said in a raised voice. 'It doesn't help you, Ian, to lash out at Gino every few minutes, even if he does provoke you. And it's getting worse.' Looking like sulky schoolboys, neither of them made any reply and Gail went on, 'Why should Sweetman's

101

crowd have known anything about your taking Jakobson's car?'

'They might have done,' Tanner said gruffly.

'In advance, you mean?'

'Could be.'

'But how, if you didn't know yourselves?'

'We'd talked about it the evening before with Mick.'

'You've never told me that.'

'No point in worrying you.'

'And even if he did find out, why should Sweetman have minded?'

'He's sort of friendly with Jakobson,' Tanner said, looking at Gino for support.

'That's right,' Gino added, nodding vigorously. 'They were specially thick at that time.'

'Yeh, they were.'

'I still don't follow it all,' Gail said in a puzzled tone. 'How could he have found out?'

'That's just what we've been trying to discover. Come on, Gail, go and get us a coffee.'

'She doesn't half ask questions,' Gino said with a sigh after she had left the room. 'Not going to tell her the whole story, are you?'

'Not likely. Not at this point. She'd tear me apart.'

'Might have been better if you had at the very beginning.'

Tanner shook his head. 'She knows as much as she needs to know.' He paused and in a change of tone, added, 'Anyway, this evening sounds like it was a real disaster.'

Gino shuddered. 'It was worse than that.'

'How'd you mean?'

'I had a row with Jeff Jakobson.'

'What about?'

'He cut up nasty when he saw me in the Knightes Bar.'

'So who cares?'

There was no answer as Gino buried his face in his

hands and gave way to a bout of violent shivering.

Ian Tanner observed him in puzzled silence. Had something else happened which Gino hadn't mentioned?

*   *   *

Philippa Chaytor went up to bed soon after eleven, which was her usual time. Her husband invariably followed her about forty minutes later, having spent the intervening period reading something for relaxation.

He was one of those people who found it impossible to read comfortably in bed. Even when the light was right, he invariably got either a crick in the neck or pins and needles in one of his arms, and, after half an hour of constantly changing his position, he had to get out and remake his side of the bed, which by then resembled a battlefield of sheets and blankets.

Philippa, on the other hand, would lie quite still on her back, one hand resting casually behind her head and the other holding a book up in the air with greater steadiness than an oak tree on a still day.

It was a quarter to midnight when Matthew Chaytor laid down the book he had been reading – one of Graham Greene's earlier novels which he had missed when it was first published – and began his round of checking doors and windows.

They lived in a much burgled area and, though they had so far escaped attention, he chose to believe this was largely due to sensible, if tiresome, precautions and not to casual oversight on the part of the burglars. Moreover, he had no desire to be put to the test of confronting one in his home in the quiet hours of the night.

Either he would put up a poor performance and thereafter feel ashamed or he might over-react and have a body in his hall, which, for a judge, would, at the very least, be embarrassing.

It had been an oppressive evening with neither of them saying very much, but with Peter's shadow dominating every room. They had eaten frugally in the kitchen alcove, as they always did when alone, and had then retired to the living-room which ran the depth of the house with windows at each end. They had watched a couple of television programmes, one of which, a documentary on market research, Philippa had found interesting while Matthew entertained searing thoughts about the excesses of the consumer society. The other had been a situation comedy which neither of them thought particularly amusing, but which, nevertheless, they lacked the will to switch off. Later, Philippa had gone to her desk to write a letter and he glanced through a number of law journals he had brought home, though with no more enthusiasm than he had shown for the television programmes.

As the evening wore on, Peter's shadow and the feeling of oppression had grown greater. Matthew would much sooner that Lorna and Douglas had come to dinner, but refrained from saying so to Philippa.

Once or twice he glanced across at her as she sat writing at her desk. They had not exchanged more than two dozen words in the past three hours. Surely, communication had not broken down between them in the way it had between him and Peter. No, the answer was that he and Philippa understood each other so well that words were often superfluous. Or so he told himself with not quite as much conviction as he would have liked. Surely he hadn't failed as a husband as well as a father? He and Philippa still made love in a satisfactory way. At least, he regarded it as such and it had never occurred to him to doubt that she felt the same. And after all, if you could still do that after twenty-three years, there couldn't be very much wrong with your marriage.

He was still indulging his introspective self when

Philippa had switched off her desk light and said she was going up to bed.

'I'll be up shortly,' he said, unnecessarily as they both knew that. Then trying to put his morbid thoughts aside, he picked up his Graham Greene and began reading.

For forty minutes or so he lost himself in the novelist's world. He reached the end of a chapter and was tempted to continue reading, but finally decided he ought to do his round of windows and doors and go up to Philippa. They invariably talked while he undressed and it was always a pleasantly relaxed few minutes. He must try and make it so even on this difficult evening.

He had reached the kitchen on his round and was double-locking the door which gave on to a side passage when a bell rang. It rang again almost immediately and then a third time as if to emphasise a sense of urgency.

He hurried from the kitchen to find Philippa already half-way down the staircase.

'It must be Peter,' she said in a tense voice.

Matthew Chaytor nodded, but on reaching the door caution compelled him to call out, 'Who's there?'

'It's me, Peter.'

Philippa stood waiting at the foot of the stairs while he slid back the bolts and turned keys in the two locks. He pulled the door open and Peter lunged inside, panting hard.

'I've run from the station,' he said between gasps, endeavouring to give his parents the semblance of a smile. 'I'll get my breath back in a moment.'

'You look as if you could do with a drink,' Matthew Chaytor said robustly. 'What shall I get you?'

But Peter shook his head. 'All I want is to go to bed,' he muttered.

'Your room's all ready, Peter,' Philippa said. 'Shall I fetch you something? A sandwich? A hot drink of some sort?'

'No, I don't want anything, mother.'

105

He made to pass her at the foot of the stairs, paused, gave her a quick peck on the cheek and went slowly up to his room.

It was not until they heard him close his bedroom door that either of them spoke.

'He looks terrible,' Matthew Chaytor said. 'I'm afraid something must have happened.'

'He did say he'd run from the station, Matt.'

'That wouldn't account for his appearance. To me, he had a frightened look.'

'I know,' Philippa said, miserably.

'We must try and get him to talk.'

'Not tonight. Let him have his sleep.'

'If past record's anything to go by, he'll stay in bed for the next twenty-four hours.'

'That's where he feels safest.'

'I daresay, but surely we have a duty to try and find out what his trouble is? I mean, supposing – though God forbid – it's something serious, we might have to take some action of our own.'

Philippa came across to where her husband was standing and rested her hands on his shoulders.

'Oh, Matt, I'm so worried about him.'

He raised his own hand and put it over one of hers in a protective gesture.

'I know you are, my love, and so am I.' But even as he spoke he realised that Philippa's anxiety was far less selfishly motivated than his. Hers was entirely on her son's account, whereas he knew that, in part at least, he was thinking of his own position.

'He hinted at problems when he phoned,' Philippa went on in a musing way, 'and now two days later he turns up. What can have happened in the interval?'

Her husband nodded. 'I know.' Then looking into her eyes, he said, 'We've got to go and talk to him. Now. If he won't say anything to us, at least we'll have tried.'

106

'Wouldn't it be better to wait until the morning?' But her tone told him she was won over.

'Come on, let's go up,' he said gently, 'before he falls asleep.'

They could see his light still shining beneath the door and Philippa knocked quietly. There was no response and she turned the handle.

Peter was lying on his back staring at the ceiling, the bedclothes pulled up under his chin. His windcheater and trousers lay in an untidy heap on the floor and his shoes gave the appearance of having been kicked off in opposite directions. It was apparent that he hadn't bothered to remove any of his other clothing.

'We felt we must talk to you, Peter, before we went to bed,' Matthew said. 'Even if we don't see you too often these days, we still worry about you.'

'You don't have to,' Peter said in a detached voice, still staring at the ceiling and without moving his head.

'Have to or not, we do. It's obvious that something's happened, so wouldn't it be better to tell us?'

'Please, Peter,' Philippa urged.

His expression, however, remained unchanged and he never shifted his gaze from the ceiling. It seemed an age before he spoke.

'I just got tired of the place I was at and decided to have a change. That's all.'

'Was that the Monkes Tale?' his father asked.

'Yes.'

'Run by a man called Jakobson?'

'Ye-es.'

'He's a witness in a case I'm trying.'

'I know.'

'Did he tell you that?'

'Yes. But he didn't know you were my father at the time.'

Matthew heaved a small sigh of relief. That, at least,

was comforting news, if it was true. He became aware of Philippa's sceptical glance and gave her a small, half-apologetic smile.

'What went wrong at the Monkes Tale, Peter?' she asked.

'I just didn't like it any more, that's all.'

'But something must have happened, darling, to make you not like it any more.'

'I got bored there.'

'What was your job?'

'Anything I was asked to do.'

'Did you come straight from there this evening?'

'Yes, no. Anyway what's it matter?'

Though his attention still remained fixed on the ceiling, his voice had become increasingly tense.

'Because your father and I want to know how best we can help you, Peter. And we can only help you, if we know what's happened.' When he made no reply, Philippa went on, 'If you're in some sort of trouble, please tell us.'

He turned his head abruptly, not in his parents' direction, but with face against the wall.

Philippa moved across to the bed and peered at him. When she returned to her husband's side, she whispered, 'He's crying.'

He gave a helpless shrug. 'We'd better leave him. Maybe, he'll feel more like talking in the morning.'

He didn't actually believe this, though with himself out of the house, it was possible that Peter might unburden himself to his mother.

From ancient habit, Philippa stooped down to pick up his clothes. She folded his trousers and hung his wind-cheater over the back of a chair. Then she retrieved his shoes and placed them beside the chair. Finally she went over to the bed and bent down to kiss him on the temple. On their way out of the room, she switched off the light.

108

'Let's hope he'll sleep,' she said in an exhausted voice, as she closed his bedroom door.

Matthew nodded. That was something he entertained no doubt about. Peter had always been able to sleep, never more so than when he was in trouble. It was, for him, as with many, the classic retreat into the womb.

*   *   *

The Canterbury Grill Room closed at midnight on the dot. The odds were that the chef had sloped off home around half past ten so that late diners were apt to be told that everything was off, save for those items which had been left to a slow process of leathery dehydration on the hot plate or which could be flambéed at the table by Raoul, the head waiter whose panache outdistanced his discretion.

Immediately after the last diner had paid his bill, it was Raoul's job to convey the evening's takings to Jeff Jakobson's office and hand them over to the proprietor. If, for any reason, Jakobson was not going to be there, he would let Raoul know and they were then locked away in the bottom drawer of Jakobson's desk, to which Raoul had a key.

But normally Jakobson himself received the money and, after checking it, locked it away in his wall safe.

Originally, this duty had fallen to the cashier, who sat at a small desk at the entrance to the grill-room, but after there had been no fewer than six cashiers in the course of a single month, Jeff Jakobson had decided that a stronger element of continuity was required and placed the duty on Raoul who had worked at the Monkes Tale for nearly two years. He also rather enjoyed a late night chat with his Spanish head waiter, who fell into the category of charming villain, but whose loyalty to his employer guaranteed his honesty where the takings were concerned.

On this particular evening, the last two diners had left soon after half past eleven, squeezed out by the inhospitable air that permeated the grill-room like a dank mist when the staff wanted to go home.

Raoul bowed them out with a barely civil smile. They had undertipped and he was not going to waste his normally effusive words of farewell on them.

The cashier had just departed, having left a note of the evening's takings, less what was paid by the last two diners. Raoul accepted their money and added it to the total. Then locking the black cash-box in which the money was kept, he picked it up and, switching off the grill-room lights, made his way to Jakobson's office.

He knocked lightly on the door, but there was no answer. He knocked again, louder this time, but there was still no reply.

Slowly he turned the handle and opened the door. There was no one inside.

He decided that Jakobson had gone to the lavatory and would be back in a couple of minutes. With this in mind, he stood in the open doorway and faced along the short corridor waiting for his employer's return. Five minutes later, he was still waiting.

Thoroughly puzzled, he entered the office and peered around cautiously, even looking beneath the desk. But there was neither any sign of Jakobson nor any clue as to where he might be.

Raoul glanced at the ashtray which was full, and sniffed. Jakobson was a heavy smoker, but the smell in his office was of stale smoke rather than of recent smoking. Raoul could only assume that his employer had been called away suddenly without time even to slip into the grill-room and tell him.

He glanced once more round the room as if Jakobson might suddenly appear out of a wall. Then with a shrug, he unlocked the desk drawer and put away the cash box.

Closing the office door behind him, he decided to have a quick look around the car park. The door at the end of the corridor which opened on to it was bolted and locked. It was the job of the cellarman to do that when the bars closed at eleven. After that hour, the only way in or out was through the main entrance at the front.

Raoul walked round to the car park and surveyed it. Two or three cars were still parked there. They probably belonged to customers who hadn't trusted themselves to drive home but who would return in the morning and retrieve their cars.

He was about to return inside when he noticed Jakobson's car parked in its usual place against the building and close to the exit door at the end of his office corridor.

Hunching his shoulders against a chill wind, he walked over to it and peered through the windows. It was empty and the doors were all locked. Moreover, the engine was quite cold.

So if Jakobson had gone anywhere, it had been in someone else's car.

With a growing sense of uneasiness, he returned inside and ran upstairs and along the corridor where Jakobson had his bedroom. He knocked on the door and opened it. The room was empty and the bed had not been slept in.

He tried to recall when he had last seen his employer. It must have been around nine o'clock. He had been standing in the entrance to the grill room when Jakobson, followed by Peter Chaytor, had walked across the hall and through the door that led to his office corridor.

Perhaps Peter knew what had happened. A few minutes later, however, he found himself gazing round an empty bedroom.

All he could do now was go to bed himself. Doubtless morning would bring its answer to Jeff Jakobson's disappearance.

But it didn't.

111

CHAPTER NINE

Shortly before nine o'clock the next morning, T.D.C. Bramley called in at the station on his way to the Old Bailey, just to scan his desk and see if there were any overnight messages.

There were none and he was about to leave again when Detective Inspector Shotter put his head round the door.

'Ah! I'm glad I caught you, Pat,' he said. 'I want you to go along to the Monkes Tale right away.'

'What about the Old Bailey, sir?'

'I'll phone and say you won't be there till later. Sergeant Griffin's finished his evidence, hasn't he? He can sit on his backside just as well as you can – even if he's not as ornamental. If I had anyone else to send I would, but I haven't. Anyway, you've more of an interest than anyone else, Jakobson having been a witness in your case.'

'Has something happened to Jakobson?'

'That'll be for you to find out. He's disappeared. Hasn't been seen since yesterday evening. Yes, I know that's not very long ago, but the person who phoned – some foreign chap – sounded pretty worried and seemed certain that his disappearance wasn't voluntary. Except that he didn't put it quite as concisely as that.'

'Was he suggesting that Jakobson had been kidnapped, sir?'

'Amongst other things, yes.'

'I see,' Patrick said thoughtfully.

'So you'd better go along there and see what you can find out. If you're satisfied there's nothing sinister about his disappearance, he can be processed as a missing person as a precaution. Then if he suddenly turns up, only the computer will get a few hiccoughs.'

'Who's in charge there now, sir?'

D.I. Shotter studied a piece of paper in his hand. 'Raoul Vicente was the name of the chap who phoned. You'd better contact him.'

Patrick's arrival at the Monkes Tale in his own mini was the reason that Raoul didn't instantly dash out and greet him. As it was, he was standing in the main entrance watching out for a police car with siren sounding and blue light flashing.

'Sorry, we are closed,' he said as Patrick made to enter. 'We do not open till half past eleven.'

'I'm Detective Constable Bramley. I gather someone phoned about Mr Jakobson.'

'You are police then?' When Patrick nodded, he said with a hasty bow, 'Oh, sorry, please you come in.'

He led the way to an alcove off the main lobby and motioned Patrick to sit down.

'Are you Raoul Vicente?' Patrick asked.

'Yes, that is me.'

'And what's your job here?'

'I'm *maitre d*' in our Canterbury Grill Room,' he said with a touching note of pride.

'Fine. Now tell me what's happened.'

To Patrick's agreeable surprise, the story came forth in intelligible sequence and without a great deal of declamation.

'And you've looked for him again this morning?'

'Everywhere we have searched.'

'You mentioned an employee who has also disappeared, what's his name?'

'Peter.'

'Peter who?'

'I do not know his other name. He did not work in grillroom.'

'What was his job?'

'He work for Mr Jakobson.'

114

'His assistant, do you mean?'

'He spend much time doing nothing.'

'And you say that the last time you saw Mr Jakobson was around nine o'clock yesterday evening?'

'Yes, he walked across the lobby here and went through that door, which leads to his office. Peter was behind him.'

'Did Peter go through the door with him?'

'No, behind him.'

Patrick smiled at the correction. It seemed that Raoul's use of English was more precise than his own.

'I'd like to see Mr Jakobson's office and while I'm doing so, perhaps you'd find out some particulars of Peter for me. His name and where he comes from. I'll also want a physical description.'

'And of Mr Jakobson?'

'I've met Mr Jakobson, so I know what he looks like.'

Raoul led him to the office and departed on his errand.

Closing the door behind him, Patrick inhaled deeply. He had always remembered being told at training school that your nose was every bit as important as your eyes when examinging any scene. What his nose told him on this occasion was that Jakobson's office smelt even nastier than the C.I.D. room at the end of a hard day.

But smell apart, nothing struck him as untoward. After letting his gaze slowly roam round, he got down on his knees to look more closely at a patch of carpet which bore faint scuff marks. They might or might not be of any significance, but he upturned the wastepaper basket and placed it over the marks to preserve them.

Still on his knees, he crawled a couple of yards over to the brick hearth. About half way along its front edge, he saw what looked like a small amount of congealed blood. Closer scrutiny made him certain that it was blood. He discovered that when he stood it was scarcely visible, being almost the same colour as the hearth itself.

Kneeling down again, he peered at it closely once more.

Yes, he had been right, there was a hair caught in the blood. He tried to see its colour, but found this was impossible without removing it. He could tell that it was dark in shade, but that was all. At all events it was not dissimilar to Jakobson's hair.

He felt a tingle of excitement, as he stepped over to the desk to telephone D.I. Shotter. It was the sort of tingle that had been in all too short supply since he joined the C.I.D., but which instantly drove out all thoughts of retirement.

While he was waiting for a reply, his eye measured the distance from the area of scuffed carpet to the bloodstained edge of the hearth. He reckoned that if someone of Jakobson's height had been standing on the first spot and had fallen backwards, his head would just about have hit the sharp edge of the brickwork where he had found the bloodstain.

If that was right, what had caused Jakobson to fall backwards? And, even more significant, what had happened to him thereafter?

His thoughts were interrupted by D.I. Shotter's voice on the line. 'Yes, Pat, what is it? Be quick about it, I've got to go out. There's been a hold-up at Parsons the jewellers. They got away with £20,000 worth of stuff.'

Quickly Patrick reported his findings.

'We'd better have someone from the lab examine the scene,' Shotter said briskly. 'Speak to Detective Chief Superintendent Eaves at division and tell him the position. Say I told you to call him. Meanwhile, make sure his office is locked and no one can get in.'

A couple of minutes later, Patrick was through to divisional headquarters. Detective Chief Superintendent Eaves had been out all night on a murder enquiry, but he was able to speak to the detective superintendent who was his second-in-command. This officer listened patiently and then said he would do his best to get an officer from the

116

lab along to the Monkes Tale as soon as possible, but could make no promises.

'They're up to their eyes at the moment,' he remarked. 'But aren't we all? I met Jakobson once at a social function. Dodgy sort of customer, I reckoned.'

Patrick agreed. As he rang off, the door opened and Raoul reappeared.

'Stop there! Don't come in any further,' he said to the startled Spaniard. 'It's just that we want to have one of our scientists examine the room and I'm going to lock it until he comes. Where's the key?'

'Mr Jakobson always has the key.'

'There must be a duplicate somewhere.'

'Perhaps Miss Joyce knows.'

At that moment, a middle-aged woman appeared in the doorway.

'Can I help? I'm Miss Joyce. I work here in the mornings and deal with the secretarial side of the establishment. I gather you're Mr Bromley.'

'Bramley. I want to lock Mr Jakobson's office, do you know if there's a spare key?'

'There should be one. We have a box of duplicates for most doors. I'll go and look if you like.'

'Thank you.'

'I just came along as I gather from Raoul that you were asking for particulars of Peter Chaytor.'

'Chaytor, did you say?'

'Yes. I understand his father's a judge, though I only learnt that a day or so ago.'

Patrick blinked in stunned surprise. He felt that events had been given a sudden jerk out of control.

'What exactly was Peter Chaytor's job here?' he asked when his tongue was working again. 'Raoul didn't seem too certain.'

'I don't think any of us were. He wasn't on the payroll, but I have reason to believe that Mr Jakobson used to

117

give him money from time to time. He had free board and lodging and used to do odd jobs for Mr Jakobson. I know about the money position, because I look after the staff records amongst other duties.' Miss Joyce cast Patrick a shrewd glance. 'To be absolutely frank with you, Mr Bramley, he always struck me as the sort of young man who was a drop-out. Not that I had anything against him.'

'When did you last see Mr Jakobson?'

'I had a brief word with him as I was leaving yesterday. That would have been about half past one. I finish officially at one and have a quick bite to eat before I go.'

'Thank you, Miss Joyce, you've been most helpful. If you could look for that spare key . . .'

'I'll do so straightaway.'

'No sooner had she gone than her place in the doorway was taken by someone else.

'I'm Phil. I'm the barman in the Knightes Bar. What's all this about Mr Jakobson disappearing? I've just arrived and heard the rumour.'

'It's more than a rumour. When did you last see him, Phil?'

'About nine o'clock. He walked through the bar followed by Peter. From their looks, they'd had, or were about to have, a good old row. They each looked about as friendly as a thunder cloud.'

'Was that unusual?'

'Fairly. Mr Jakobson could turn nasty quite quickly. You know, all good fellowship one minute and a vicious kick in the goolies the next. Actually, I reckon yesterday was his bad day. He'd had a row earlier in the evening with a customer.'

'What about?'

'It was a young chap he'd warned off the premises months ago after he'd had his car nicked and smashed up. He wasn't too pleased seeing him here last night and they flung a few words at each other.'

118

'Threats?'

'You could call them that, I suppose.'

'What was the customer's name?'

'Gino. Don't know his other name.'

'Gino Evans?' Patrick asked keenly.

'Could be. He was a friend of the chap who's on trial.'

'That's Gino Evans.' After a slight pause, Patrick said, 'Did you see Peter again yesterday evening?'

'No.'

'Thanks for coming along. I'll need to get a signed statement from you later.'

'You know where to find me. In ye olde Knightes Bar,' he said, giving Patrick a broad wink as he turned to go.

Mr Littledale of the Metropolitan Police Laboratory turned up much sooner than Patrick had expected. He explained that he had been completing his evidence in a case at Kingston Crown Court and had received a message telling him to call at the Monkes Tale on his way back into town.

'That's blood all right,' he said, after examining the stain on the brick hearth. He carefully scraped it into a plastic envelope, together with the hair. He then collected particles of debris from where the carpet had been scuffed. 'Anything else?' he enquired, looking around the room.

'Nothing that I've noticed,' Patrick remarked.

Mr Littledale, however, made his own examination before being satisfied. 'I suppose I'd better empty the ashtray,' he remarked. 'You may want to know how many different people smoked in here yesterday. Saliva tests can help tell us that.' When he had finished, he said, 'Now, control samples. Obviously, we can't get hold of his blood, but there should be some hairs in his comb or on some of his clothing. Let's go up to his bedroom.'

Patrick watched while he trotted about the bedroom with the enthusiasm of a terrier. Although the comb yielded a fine harvest of hairs, he wasn't satisfied until he had found others on a jacket in the wardrobe.

'Just as well to have two sources,' he observed cheerfully. 'You never know, he may have lent his comb to someone.'

'I wouldn't have thought of that,' Patrick said, admiringly.

'Nor would I if I hadn't been fooled once before. And oh, what a lot of trouble I brought on myself on that occasion!'

After Mr Littledale had departed with his collection of samples, Patrick rang his station. But D.I. Shotter was still out and there was no answer on any of the C.I.D. extensions, so he left a message with an officer on the front desk saying that he was on his way to the Old Bailey.

Until Jakobson turned up, alive or dead, there wasn't a great deal more that could be done. Indeed, Patrick could think of only one further enquiry to undertake.

Namely to find and interview Peter Chaytor.

CHAPTER TEN

When Matthew Chaytor left for court, his son was still
in bed. Philippa had tiptoed into his room and emerged
to say that he was fast asleep.

'If anything happens,' Matthew said, 'phone me immediately at the Old Bailey.'

'How do I get hold of you in court?'

'Tell the telephonist you want to speak to me urgently
and someone will let me know. I'll warn her that you may
be calling.'

'I hope it won't be necessary, Matt.'

'So do I, but the possibility has to be faced. He's obviously in trouble of some sort. Serious trouble to judge
by his arrival last night; so we must be prepared for something to happen. If it's the police who call, don't answer
any questions or let them talk to Peter until you've phoned
me. Just find out what they want and get in touch straight
away.'

Philippa nodded. She knew that he was partially moti-
vated by self-interest, but was in no mood to accuse him.
She was grateful for support from any quarter where
Peter's welfare was concerned.

As Matthew Chaytor settled himself in his seat and
looked quickly round the court-room, he noticed that the
young police officer who had been attending the trial was
absent, his place taken by the uniformed sergeant who had
given evidence the previous day. But he attached no significance to the fact.

'Yes, Mr Batchford, you were in the middle of your
client's examination-in-chief when we adjourned yesterday.'

In fact defending counsel had very little more to ask Tanner. Sometimes it was helpful to recapitulate certain evidence when there had been a break, just to remind the jury of the bits you wished them to remember, but he lacked the necessary confidence in his client to risk it in this case. He hadn't spoken to Tanner since he had begun his evidence and didn't put it beyond him to ride off on a new tack if given half a chance. Particularly after a night in which to think about it.

'You were saying when we adjourned yesterday that you were in a state of shock after the accident?'

'S'right.'

'And remember very little of what you did?'

'Don't remember anything much.'

'I think it was two days later that Sergeant Griffin called to see you at Miss Norbet's flat?'

'Yeh.'

'And asked you to accompany him to the police station?'

'S'right.'

'And you did so?'

'Yeh.'

'Quite voluntarily?'

'Didn't have any choice, did I?'

'Anyway, you didn't object?'

'No. No point, was there?'

'Did the officer caution you?'

'I don't remember. If he says he did, I suppose he must have done.'

'According to Sergeant Griffin, you declined to say anything, is that correct?'

'Yeh.'

'Why?'

'Because I was still all shocked by what had happened. My mind was all a haze.'

'So you decided to stay silent?'

'It was my right, wasn't it?'

Judge Chaytor turned in Tanner's direction. 'Do you think you could give your evidence without adding a question to the end of every answer?'

Ian Tanner gave him a blank look.

'Sorry, I don't get you.'

'You said, "it was my right, wasn't it?" and before that, "didn't have any choice, did I?" '

'Well I didn't, did I?'

'There, you did it again! Just try and answer the questions without asking your own.'

'O.K.'

'I haven't very much more I wish to ask you,' Batchford remarked for the benefit of both his client and the judge. 'But tell me this, how long had you known Burleigh?'

'Three or four years.'

'How close were you to him?'

'He was one of my mates.'

'Will you ever be able to forget the horror of that night?'

The judge gave defending counsel a pained look, but refrained from any comment.

'Never. It's like a sort of nightmare.'

Andrew Batchford resumed his seat, and Mr Ridge sprang up with an alacrity that took everyone by surprise.

'When did you first learn, Tanner, that your mate, Burleigh, was the victim?'

'I don't remember,' Tanner replied, nervously.

'Don't remember?' Mr Ridge said sharply.

'No.'

'Was it before the police saw you?'

'Yes.'

'Not much thought of his being your mate then, was there?'

'I don't follow.'

'For at least forty-eight hours, you had an opportunity of going to the police and didn't. That's right, isn't it?' Mr Ridge barked.

'I've explained. I was shocked.'

'Not so shocked that you didn't try and hide the car and make a bee-line for your girl-friend's flat, eh?'

'Mr Ridge,' the judge broke in, 'it'll be easier for the witness and the jury if you ask one question at a time.' He felt like adding, and refrain from using such a hectoring tone.

'You hid the car, didn't you?'

'I . . .'

'Hid it in the trees, eh?'

'I didn't hide it.'

'And went straight to your girl-friend's?'

'Yes.'

'Not much sign of shock, eh?'

'I was shocked.'

'Not much sign of it, though, eh?'

'My girl-friend'll support me.'

'You never really believed that Mr Jakobson wouldn't mind your taking his car, did you?'

'Yes.'

'I put it to you that you didn't?'

'I did.'

'You just took it, didn't you?'

'I've explained . . .'

'Didn't you?'

'No.'

'I put it to you, you did?'

'No.'

'And you were driving at at least fifty or sixty miles an hour in Waterworks Lane, weren't you?'

'No.'

'I put it to you, you were?'

'No.'

'You knew the police were chasing you?'

'I thought I'd thrown them off by then.'

'I suggest you knew they were still on your tail?'

'No.'

'Are you sticking to that answer?'

'Yes.'

Whatever Andrew Batchford had expected of his opponent's style of cross-examination, it had not been the excitably flung questions that had come from Mr Ridge. It was as if someone of erratic aim was pelting another with anything that came to hand, rotten fruit, old cans, pebbles and the odd hefty lump of rock.

'You deliberately crossed the lights at red, didn't you?'

'No.'

'I put it to you, you did?'

'No.'

'I put it to you that your whole evidence is a farrago of lies?'

Andrew Batchford groaned inwardly as he tried to decide whether to intervene. In the event, he was beaten to it by the judge.

'Do you really mean the *whole* of his evidence, Mr Ridge?'

'All the important parts, my lord.'

'And who's saying which those parts are?'

'I'm sure the witness knows what I mean, my lord,' Mr Ridge said boldly.

'Well, I don't and I doubt very much if the jury do.'

'And I don't either,' Andrew Batchford murmured.

For a moment, Mr Ridge resembled a penguin at bay. Then glaring at Tanner he said, 'You've lied about everything that matters, haven't you?'

'No. I've told the truth.'

'You don't know what the truth is, do you?'

'Yes.'

'Then why haven't you told it?'

'I have.'

'I put it to you that your evidence is a tissue of lies from beginning to end?'

125

'No.'

'Is that your final answer?'

'Yes.'

Perspiring freely Mr Ridge sat down with the exhausted but satisfied air of one who has scaled forensic heights.

To Andrew Batchford it had exceeded the legal saw that to cross-examine did not mean to examine crossly. Prosecuting counsel had not only managed to sound testy, but had combined it with futility.

It was during the closing stages of the cross-examination that T.D.C. Bramley had come into court and slipped into a seat beside Sergeant Griffin. It was shortly afterwards that Matthew Chaytor found himself being stared at in a very strange way.

On the basis that re-examination of a witness is the process by which his credibility is restored after cross-examination, Andrew Batchford decided that he had no further questions to ask his client. Ian Tanner's credibility was still intact. Or, rather, no less intact than it had ever been.

'Then I think we'll adjourn,' the judge said. 'I know it's a bit early, but I have a personal matter I must attend to.' As he spoke he became aware of the young officer still giving him the strangest of looks.

Patrick had decided that he must report Jakobson's mysterious disappearance to Mr Ridge and rather hoped he could let defending counsel know at the same time. He had no intention, however, of mentioning Peter Chaytor's name.

His opportunity came when he observed the two barristers in conversation as they prepared to leave court.

' 'Fraid I had to tear into your chap a bit,' Mr Ridge was saying as Patrick approached. 'Pile into them and don't give them time to recover is my maxim when cross-examining.'

'I don't know about recover, you scarcely gave him

126

time to answer,' Andrew Batchford observed drily.

'With all respect to you, Batchford, a client like yours really doesn't know what truth means. Could anyone believe the tale he spun?'

'That we shall find out in due course. Though, given two of your witnesses, it does seem to be a case of the pot calling the kettle black.'

'I agree Jakobson wasn't too impressive, but I thought Cox was a first-rate witness.'

'Really?'

'Oh, yes. He may have a bit of a criminal record, but, if you ask me, his evidence was as truthful as the day is long. I'm sure the jury were impressed by him.'

'Hmm!' was Andrew Batchford's only comment. Then his eyes brightened as he became aware of Patrick's presence. 'I saw you coming in late trying to look unobtrusive,' he said, with a smile.

'I was out on an enquiry. It's something I think I ought to mention to you two gentlemen. Jeff Jakobson has disappeared. He's been missing since yesterday evening.'

'Is foul play suspected?' Mr Ridge enquired solemnly.

'It's too early to say, but it can't be ruled out.'

'Ought we to tell the judge?' Mr Ridge asked, looking at Andrew Batchford.

Defending counsel was thoughtful for a few seconds. 'Yes, I think he probably should be told. I don't know that it'll do him much good, but he might be annoyed if he subsequently learnt that we had known and not told him. After all, he's going to have to deal with Jakobson's evidence when he sums up to the jury.'

Patrick said nothing. It was not for him to voice doubts about the wisdom of telling the judge anything, though it did seem to him most irregular for a judge to try a case in which he had the sort of interest that Judge Chaytor had.

'Shall we go and see him together?' Mr Ridge now asked.

'Good heavens no! You can tell him. After all, Jakobson was your witness and Mr Bramley is, strictly speaking, reporting to you. In one sense, I've merely eavesdropped.'

'I take your point, Batchford,' Mr Ridge said in a pompous voice. 'I'll see if I can catch him now.' He glanced doubtfully at the deserted bench. 'Actually, how do I find him?'

'I suggest you go through that door and speak to an usher in the judge's corridor.'

'Right.'

A couple of minutes later on making known his wish to one of the ushers, he was directed to Judge Chaytor's room. He was about to knock on the door when he heard voices inside the room. He cocked an ear and realised it was the judge talking on the telephone.

'Still asleep?' he heard the judge say in a weary tone.

There followed further words which he couldn't hear and then the short ping of the bell as the receiver was replaced.

Taking a deep breath, he knocked and heard the judge call out 'come in'.

'Yes, Ridge, what is it?' Judge Chaytor said as his visitor entered. Quickly he added, 'But before you answer that, are you sure you're behaving properly in coming to see me on your own?'

'Batchford knows about it, judge,' Mr Ridge replied in a slightly hurt tone. 'In fact, it was his suggestion.'

'I see. What is it then?'

'It's about the witness, Jakobson. He's disappeared in slightly mysterious circumstances, it seems.'

To Ridge's astonishment, the judge's face became drained of colour and he grasped the arms of his chair tightly so that his knuckles shone through the tautened skin.

128

'Are you feeling all right, judge?' he stammered.

'Yes, I'm perfectly all right, thank you,' Matthew Chaytor said in a tone that conveyed his irritation at the question. 'What are the so called mysterious circumstances?' he went on, in a voice tightly under control.

'Detective Constable Bramley says he's been missing since yesterday evening and the police are not ruling out the possibility of foul play.'

'I see.'

'Of course, he's completed his evidence and I don't myself see that his disappearance affects my case at all, but after discussing the matter with Batchford we decided it was right to let you know. For what it's worth,' he added with a short barking laugh.

'I'm glad you did,' Matthew Chaytor replied.

Mr Ridge hovered uncertainly for a few seconds. 'Well, if that's all, judge, I won't disturb you further.'

The judge gave him an abstracted nod and, after hovering a bit longer as though waiting for a tip, he turned and left the room.

As he walked back along the judge's corridor, he wondered whether he ought to inform someone that Judge Chaytor seemed unwell. He decided, however, that this might appear officious. The judge had only to press a bell if he wanted assistance.

In fact Matthew Chaytor did press his bell shortly after prosecuting counsel had left him. When an usher came, he said, 'Somewhere in this building, there's a Detective Constable Bramley. At least, I expect he's still in the building, probably in the police room. I shall be grateful if you will find him and ask him to come and have a word with me.' He gave the usher a wan smile. 'I hope it won't be quite as bad as searching for a needle in a haystack.'

The usher's expression remained inscrutable, however, as he retired from the room.

Matthew Chaytor shook his head slowly in silent

thought. No wonder that young officer had looked at him in such a strange manner. He obviously knew about Peter. As far as the police were concerned Peter had also disappeared, though it seemed that he hadn't mentioned this aspect to the two counsel. That, at any rate, was one crumb of comfort. If he had told them, it was inconceivable that the insensitive Ridge would not have mentioned this, too. He glanced at his watch. There were still ten minutes to go before the normal hour of adjournment. He was sure he was being given black marks in every quarter for indulging his personal convenience in this way. A new judge, sitting at the Old Bailey for the first time, behaving like the worst sort of judicial despot. He couldn't really blame anyone if they were thinking that. It had been a ghastly morning, waiting minute by minute to be called to the telephone, trying to concentrate on the proceedings in court and, on top of all that, having to endure prosecuting counsel's abysmal cross-examination. He looked at his watch again. One thing for sure he would once more be forgoing lunch with his fellow judges. Moreover, if he had to delay his return to court after the adjournment he would not hesitate to do so. It would all depend on how quickly Detective Constable Bramley could be located and what he had to say. Or more precisely what he was prepared to say.

Patrick was standing in line for food at the cafeteria when the usher found him.

'You Detective Constable Bramley?' he asked gloomily, after Patrick had been pointed out to him.

'Yes.'

'Judge Chaytor wants to see you.'

'See me?' Patrick said in a startled tone.

'That's what he says.'

Patrick lowered his empty tray and dangled it at his side.

'If you want to have something to eat, I'll tell him I

couldn't find you,' the usher said in the same mournful tone.

'No, I suppose I'd better come. But thanks all the same. Where is he?'

'In his room. I'll show you.'

As they traipsed along corridors and down a couple of flights of stairs, Patrick had time to think what he should say. Though he had been startled by the summons, he reflected that it shouldn't have come as that much of a surprise. After all, he had known that the judge was going to be told about Jakobson's disappearance and he obviously knew about his son's employment at the Monkes Tale. The question was, what else did he know?

'Third door on the right,' the usher said waving a hand down a seemingly endless corridor of soft carpet.

'Come in,' the judge called out when Patrick knocked. 'Ah! They managed to find you,' he said as Patrick entered. 'Come in and sit down. Smoke if you want to.'

'I don't, sir.'

'Sensible fellow.' Judge Chaytor, who had risen when Patrick came in, now settled himself back in his desk chair. His cupped hands rested on the desk, but appeared to be keeping time with a piece of unheard music. It seemed an age before he spoke again. 'I realise this is a somewhat unusual interview, but we're dealing with unusual circumstances,' he said at last. After a further pause he went on, 'I take it that you probably have more than an inkling what I want to talk about?'

'I may have, sir.'

'My son?'

'Yes.'

'He worked at the Monkes Tale.'

'I know, sir,' Patrick said in a stony voice.

'Not that I knew until after this trial had begun.' Patrick blinked in surprise. 'Needless to say, I wouldn't have dreamt of trying the case if I'd known beforehand.'

131

'No, of course not, sir.'

'From the way you were looking at me in court this morning, I suspect you thought otherwise.'

Patrick felt himself blushing, but decided it was safer to say nothing. It was one of those situations which are usually made worse by efforts at explanation.

'I'm afraid my son has been one of society's drop-outs. He hasn't lived at home for several years and he's not very good at keeping in touch.' He paused and added drily, 'And that's an understatement.'

'I understand, sir.'

'It's more than I do,' Matthew Chaytor said wearily. 'However, I mustn't burden you with my family troubles. I gather from counsel that Jakobson has disappeared and that there's a possibility of foul play. Are you in a position to tell me why you suspect that? Before you say anything, please understand that I'm not pressing you to say anything you shouldn't. I realise you're in a delicate position, just as I am myself.'

'It seems, sir, that Jakobson disappeared from the Monkes Tale between nine o'clock and shortly before midnight He didn't tell anyone he was going out and no one appears to have seen him leave the premises. Moreover, his car's still there. He's just vanished without trace.'

'You think he may have been abducted?'

'It's possible, sir.'

Matthew Chaytor frowned. 'Having said I didn't want to press you, it's just what I'm doing, but have you some further reason for thinking that harm may have befallen him?'

'There were certain indications in his office, sir,' Patrick said cautiously.

'I see. Incidentally, I take it you've been personally involved in the enquiries?'

'Yes, sir. That's why I was late coming to court this morning.'

'And, of course, you must have learnt that my son worked for this man?'

'Yes, sir, though only this morning.'

'Are you looking for Peter?'

So he also knows his son is missing, Patrick thought.

'We should certainly like to interview him, sir.'

'With what object in view?'

'Finding out what he can tell us about Jakobson's disappearance.'

'You think he ought to be able to help you over that?' the judge said in a tone in which each word seemed to be carefully weighed.

'Yes, sir.'

'May I enquire why?'

'Because, sir, he was the last person seen with Jakobson,' Patrick said flatly.

'Then I can certainly see why you need to see him. Have you launched a hue and cry for him yet?'

'Not yet, sir.'

'No steps have yet been taken to find him?'

'No, sir, but I have the impression that you know where he is.'

'I do, but why are you so sure?'

'Because you knew he'd disappeared before I had time to mention it. You asked me if we were looking for him.'

Matthew Chaytor gave Patrick a small nod. 'It was quick of you to spot that. I needn't give you two guesses as to where he is. He arrived on our doorstep around midnight, but he has told us nothing. I knew nothing of Jakobson's disappearance until counsel came to see me half an hour ago. And I had no idea that Peter was the last person to be seen with him until you told me.'

'What did your son tell you then?' Patrick asked, like a dog picking up a scent.

'Very little, indeed. Just that he'd got tired of working

133

at the Monkes Tale and had decided to come home for a bit.'

'How did he appear, sir?'

Matthew Chaytor shook his head wearily. 'Before we go any further, I think we'd better define the basis of our discussion. May I take it that we're talking off the record?'

Patrick swallowed nervously. He had no idea whether he had any authority to agree, but he knew that if he said no, that would be an end to their talk. It was clearly better to say 'yes' and hope for the best. He nodded his assent.

'He arrived panting and out of breath just as I was locking up and preparing to go to bed. My wife had already gone upstairs. He said he'd run from the station. He refused food or drink and went straight up to his room, which, incidentally, my wife keeps in readiness for him. We followed him up and tried to find out if he was in any trouble, but he obviously didn't want to talk and in the end we gave up and went to bed. This morning when I left home, he was still asleep.'

'How did you come to learn, sir, that he was working at the Monkes Tale?'

'He phoned my wife the day the trial started and mentioned it then. He hadn't been in touch with us for a couple of months or more before that day. You can imagine my surprise, nay shock, when my wife told me. The very day Jakobson had been in the box.'

'When will it be possible to interview him, sir?'

'You have your duty to perform and obviously the sooner the better from your point of view. Certainly I'm not going to put any obstacles in your path.' He became lost in thought for a time. Then fixing Patrick with a steady gaze, he went on, 'I think there's only one solution. I won't sit this afternoon and I'll take you back to my home immediately I have made the necessary arrangements. I must phone my wife and also let the clerk of the court know that I shan't be sitting. I shall say that urgent per-

134

sonal business has come up and regretfully the trial must be adjourned until tomorrow. I expect you'll wish to speak to your superiors before we leave?'

Patrick nodded. The judge didn't seem to envisage any hitch from the police side, but Patrick was less sure. On the other hand, D.I. Shotter might feel that events had gone too far to revoke the arrangement.

'Meet me in the judges' car park at half past two. That should give us both time to do what's necessary.'

As he left the judge's room, Patrick began to wonder whether Judge Chaytor had not deliberately rushed him into the arrangement, thinking, perhaps, that it would be better for his son to be interviewed by a young, inexperienced officer than by someone tougher and more senior. Someone who, he might think, would be less awed by the judicial presence than T.D.C. Bramley. Not that Patrick felt he had given any indication of being overawed.

He decided that it would be better not to return to court to hear the adjournment announced. There was bound to be a buzz of speculation and he had no wish to be embarrassed by anything either counsel might say to him.

He put through a call to his station and caught D.I. Shotter just as he was about to go out again. He explained the situation as briefly as he could.

'Yes, go and get a statement from him,' Shotter said when he'd finished. 'If he was the last person to see Jakobson, he's got to be interviewed. He should be able to throw some light on his disappearance. Incidentally, I suspect Billy Cox was involved in this hold-up at Parsons this morning. Probably Totty Sweetman, too. We've found the getaway car. A Jaguar nicked from outside a house late last night. Owner flew to Paris two days ago and returned this morning.'

'What makes you suspect Cox, sir?'

'Someone answering his description called at the house yesterday to enquire if the owner would like his car washed.

135

The daily woman politely told him the owner was away in Paris.'

'A good description, is it?'

D.I. Shotter gave a hollow laugh. 'Good, except for the colour of his hair. If it was Cox, he was obviously wearing a wig and has shaved off his beard. The man's lovely red curly hair impressed the dear lady no end.'

'So it mightn't have been him at all, sir.'

'That's right, Pat, but my suspicions don't go away quite so easily.'

Shortly afterwards, Patrick found his way to the judge's car park and leaned against a wall while he waited. It was a comfortable position and he welcomed the opportunity of some quiet reflection on what had happened. He found himself instead, however, thinking of Jennie and wondering if she could ever become a policeman's wife. He supposed the question would eventually resolve itself by his deciding how committed he was to his career and, of course, by her deciding just how much she wanted to become his wife. But contemplation of marriage was altogether premature. Well, *he* thought so, but he wasn't so sure about Jennie. He must try and get round and see her this evening, even if it was too late to take her out. She couldn't fail to be impressed by his day's activity.

Judge Chaytor came out of the building and indicated his car by a wave of the hand. It was a Rover 2000. The perfect car for judges, Patrick reflected as he walked over. Respectable and unostentatious. You wouldn't expect to see them driving around in some sleek ten or fifteen thousand pound job with as much gadgetry on board as a missile-carrier.

He got in beside the judge and fastened the seat belt, after observing that the judge had adjusted his.

'I'm glad to see you wear a seat belt,' Matthew Chaytor remarked as they drove off. 'I leave it to my passengers to decide for themselves, but personally I think they're a good thing. I'm afraid my wife flatly refuses ever to wear one. I suppose you're obliged to in order to set an example to the rest of us.' He tut-tutted as a young man dived from the kerb on their left to cross the road, causing at least two other cars as well as Judge Chaytor's to brake sharply and one of the drivers to give an angry blast on his horn. 'I'd like to make it an offence to sound your horn merely as an indication of annoyance or frustration.' He threw Patrick a small smile. 'Though I concede it would be a difficult law to enforce.'

For the remainder of their twenty-five minutes' journey, the conversation stayed on the same innocuous plane. Patrick had realised at an early stage that the judge wished to keep off more sensitive topics.

They arrived outside a three-storey Victorian house in one of the roads off Haverstock Hill. It was detached and smaller than its neighbours which had long since been converted into flats.

Patrick stood on the pavement staring at it while Matthew Chaytor locked the car doors, before leading the way up the short pathway to the front door which was at the top of four steps. He opened the door with a key and almost immediately a woman came into the hall from what Patrick guessed was the living-room.

'This is my wife,' the judge said.

'Detective Constable Bramley,' Patrick said, when the judge's introduction stopped short.

Mrs Chaytor shook hands. She was a large woman with pretty, honey-coloured hair pulled into a small neat bun. Her face had a smooth, if slightly puffy, appearance and Patrick reckoned she had once been extremely attractive. She still had a very good figure by his standards.

'Where's Peter?' her husband asked.

'He's down in the kitchen.'

'You've told him that an officer was coming?'

She nodded. There was an awkward silence and then

137

Matthew Chaytor said to Patrick, 'Will you excuse us a moment? I'd just like to have a word with my wife.'

They went into the living-room and closed the door, leaving Patrick standing in the hall. It was one of those houses with a semi-basement and the kitchen was obviously located there. No sound came from below and he wondered what Peter Chaytor was doing, assuming he hadn't slipped out and over the garden wall when he heard their arrival. He wondered what the judge's reaction would be if that had happened.

While he stood there, a black cat appeared from nowhere and rubbed itself against his legs.

'Whom are you bringing luck to?' he asked, as he stooped down to stroke it.

Half a minute later, the living-room door opened and the Chaytors came out.

'I'll take you down to the kitchen,' the judge said. 'Incidentally, in case you're wondering, I don't propose to remain while you interview Peter. I suspect that he would find that as inhibiting as you would. My wife and I'll be up here if you want us.'

'Thank you, sir,' Patrick said as he followed the judge down the stairs.

Sitting in the dining alcove on the farther side of the kitchen was a bearded young man, hunched over a newspaper which was spread over the table in front of him.

'Peter, this is Detective Constable Bramley who wants to ask you a few questions about events at the Monkes Tale last night,' Judge Chaytor said as they entered the kitchen.

Not until they had crossed to the alcove did Peter Chaytor look up, but he said nothing.

'I'll go back upstairs,' his father said. 'I'll see you before you leave, Bramley.'

Patrick pulled a chair out from the table and sat down opposite Peter.

138

'You know why I'm here?'

'My mother told me,' he said in a tense voice.

'You appear to be the last person to have seen Jakobson before his disappearance.'

'I don't know anything about his disappearance. I didn't even know he had disappeared until my father phoned my mother.'

'Why did you leave in such a hurry yourself?'

'I didn't. I'd got tired of the place and decided to come home.' His tone was nervous and he fiddled with his beard as he spoke.

'You can't really expect me to believe that, Peter. However tired of it you were, you'd hardly walk out late at night without a word to anyone.'

'But I would. I'm like that. Anyway, there was no reason why I should have told anyone. I wasn't on the staff.'

'Wouldn't you even have told Jakobson?'

Peter Chaytor hesitated. 'I did tell him,' he muttered, shifting his gaze to the paper on the table.

If that isn't true, Patrick reflected, it must mean that he knows Jakobson is dead and that his lie can never be disproved.

'What was his reaction when you told him?'

'He didn't mind. He knew I wanted to leave.'

'Did you have a row with him last night?'

Peter Chaytor's nervousness seemed to increase, manifested by the agitated manner he plucked at his beard.

'Who says I had a row with him?'

'Did you? That's the question!'

'No, why should we have had a row?'

'There are two witnesses who say that neither of you looked in the best of moods when last seen.'

'He'd been a bit cross with me,' Peter Chaytor said reluctantly. 'I'd been stopped for speeding by some of your lot when I was driving his car.'

139

'That all?'

'There'd been some whisky in the back that the police asked questions about. Jeff was annoyed about that, too.'

Patrick decided that Peter Chaytor had told him this as it could only be a matter of time before he found out anyway.

'So you had grounds for a row?'

'I tell you we never had a row.'

'Supposing I tell *you* that someone heard you rowing in his office?'

For a second it appeared that Peter Chaytor was going to fall sideways off his chair, but he put a hand on to the table to steady himself.

Whatever his answer, Patrick was now certain that there'd been a row. It had been a long shot and something of a cheat as he had no evidence to support his question. But police interrogations often fell into the same category as love and war.

Leaving his question unanswered, Patrick went on, 'How did you get home last night?'

'By bus and Tube,' Peter Chaytor said suspiciously.

'Do you have a car?'

'No.'

'What time did you leave the Monkes Tale?'

'I don't know.'

'About when?'

'I can't tell you. I got here about midnight.'

'Did you come direct?'

'As direct as public transport allows.'

'How long do you reckon the journey to have taken?'

'It seemed ages.'

'Over an hour?'

'Yes, at least two hours. I had to wait a long time for a bus. Then I had to change and finally I had to wait another age for a tube.'

'Where was Jakobson when you last saw him?'

'In his office.'

'Doing what?'

'Sitting at his desk.'

'How long were you in his office when you accompanied him there at nine o'clock?'

'I don't know. Perhaps half an hour.'

'What were you talking about?'

'About my leaving.'

'For a whole half-hour?'

'It may have been less.'

'And when you left his office, where did you go?'

'I went up to my room to collect my jacket and left.'

'Did you speak to anyone after leaving the office?'

'No.'

'Did you see anyone?'

'I don't think so.'

'That means you must have left by the side door at the end of Jakobson's office corridor?'

'Yes.'

'Why go that way to your room? It's longer than going through the main lobby.'

'I didn't want to meet anyone.'

'Why not?'

'Because . . . because I didn't want to stop and say good-bye to anyone.'

Peter Chaytor had shown increasing signs of fluster under Patrick's persistent questioning. Nevertheless, Patrick could not for the life of him think how he could have disposed of Jakobson's body, if, as Patrick now believed probable, he had killed him in the course of a quarrel. The alternative was that Chaytor had told the truth and really did have nothing to do with Jakobson's disappearance. But if he behaved as nervously as that when he told the truth, what was he like when he embarked on lies? And, anyway, it was inconceivable that Jakobson's

141

disappearance and Peter Chaytor's flight from the Monkes Tale were not connected.

For the moment, however, Patrick didn't see that he could take the matter any further. There was certainly no evidence on which he could arrest Chaytor. Come to that there wasn't even any evidence of an offence having been committed. It was still possible that Jakobson would turn up somewhere alive and unharmed. Indeed, with someone as slippery as he, such a possibility must linger for quite a time. It was certainly not beyond belief that he had engineered his own disappearance for some devious purpose or another.

'Are you going to stay at home, Peter?' Chaytor shrugged. 'Because this enquiry's in its infancy and I shall want to see you again. Is there anything else you'd like to tell me now?' He shook his head as though in a dream. 'Well, don't go and do anything silly like disappearing. It won't do you any good. It'll merely arouse police suspicions.'

Patrick got up, but Peter Chaytor's eyes remained fixed on the spread-out newspaper. He was still plucking nervously at his beard when Patrick reached the kitchen door and glanced back at him.

Judge Chaytor had heard Patrick's footsteps and was in the hall by the time he reached the top of the stairs.

He gave Patrick a questioning look.

'He says he doesn't know anything about Jakobson's disappearance,' Patrick said in a carefully neutral tone.

'That's what he told my wife when she said you were coming to interview him.'

It still doesn't make it true, Patrick felt like saying but didn't.

'Was he able to help you at all?' the judge went on in a worried tone.

'Not very much, sir. In fact, hardly at all.'

'So what's your next move?'

'We go on with our enquiries until we find Jakobson. If he's alive, that could be the end of the matter, but if he's not . . .'

'You'll be at the beginning of another enquiry.'

'Precisely.'

'I imagine in either case you'll probably want to see Peter again?'

'Yes, sir.'

'Have you told him so?'

'Yes. I asked him if he was proposing to stay at home, but his answer wasn't very definite.'

Matthew Chaytor sighed. 'We can hardly keep him under lock and key in our own home, but we'll certainly try and persuade him not to leave. He is apt to take off without warning, though.' He was thoughtful for a moment. 'On the other hand, I wouldn't expect him to skip away just yet. His sudden arrival late last night was very much that of someone seeking comfort and sanctuary and I doubt whether the mood has worn off, or will for at least a few days.' He stared pensively at the Chinese rug on the hall floor. 'I must in fairness to Peter tell you that his arrival was nothing out of the ordinary for him. He's done it on previous occasions. Pressures build up and he takes refuge at home until he feels able to cope with life again. I'm sure you've come across the pattern before. The young of today seem particularly prone to it. All these nervous breakdowns, suicides, drug addictions, they're all part of it. Everyone has his theory as to the reasons, but the reality is all around us. There's Peter what he is and there's you a keen, industrious young police officer playing a useful role in society.' He shook his head forlornly. 'The point I'm really making is that Peter's homecoming doesn't necessarily mean he's done anything wrong, anything against the law, that is. Moreover, it would be quite out of pattern for him to have committed any really serious criminal offence, particularly one involving violence.' He

143

fixed Patrick with a steady look. 'If something *has* happened to Jakobson, I'm sure it must have occurred to you that Peter couldn't possibly have disposed of the body. Apart from it being totally out of character, he simply wouldn't have had the means.'

Patrick nodded, though as non-committally as a nod could be made. He only accepted the last part of the judge's view, for he still didn't see how Peter Chaytor could have spirited Jakobson away from the Monkes Tale, either dead or alive.

'I'd better be getting back to my station, sir,' he said, making a move toward the front door. 'Will you be sitting tomorrow?'

A cloud passed over the judge's face. 'As far as I know, yes. I must consider the position and, perhaps, have a word with one of my brother judges. My feeling at the moment is that I can continue trying the case, even though my strong personal inclination would be to discharge the jury and order a re-trial. But I must have regard to the inconvenience that would cause and also to the waste of public money and time.' He paused, hand on door latch, 'Once there is the faintest suggestion that Peter has been involved in some criminal act against Jakobson, I must abort the trial, but, until that moment and having regard to the distance it's already gone, I feel my public duty requires me to continue.' He gave Patrick a wan smile. 'Anyway, that's how I see it at the moment.'

It was obvious to Patrick that he didn't know about his son's brush with the law over suspect whisky and speeding in Jakobson's car and Patrick decided it wasn't his business to tell him. It was something he would be looking into himself as soon as he got back to the station. And, anyway, these were not offences against Jakobson such as might influence the judge to abandon the trial. Rather, they seemed to be offences committed with Jakobson's connivance.

144

Judge Chaytor opened the front door and Patrick stepped outside. As he turned to murmur his good-bye, the judge said, 'I should like to thank you for having been considerate as well as co-operative.'

Which was more than Patrick felt he could say for Peter Chaytor. There had been little co-operation from that quarter.

CHAPTER ELEVEN

It was nearly five o'clock when Patrick Bramley returned to his station. Detective Constable Wain was the only occupant of their room.

'The D.I. was asking if you were back,' Wain said. 'Better watch out, he's on a short fuse. He could blow up any moment so I hope you take him good news.'

'I don't.'

'Well, handle carefully and stand back,' Wain said, returning his attention to the typewriter on which he was laboriously picking out with two heavy fingers a report on a case of indecent assault.

'The red-haired car washer wasn't Cox after all,' D.I. Shotter said before Patrick was halfway through his door. He spoke in a tone of disgust as if he had been deprived of his rightful prey. 'We found him washing a car in a neighbouring street this afternoon. He was able to satisfy us that he had nothing to do with the theft of the Jaguar.'

In view of the warning he had received from D.C. Wain, Patrick refrained from saying it had struck him as unlikely that Cox, even a disguised Cox, would go calling at the house outside which he was proposing to steal a car. It seemed an unnecessary risk. There were other, more discreet, ways of finding out whether the owner of a car was away from home.

'Do you still suspect the Sweetman gang, sir?'

'It was their m.o. all right, nicking a car the night before a job, in particular a car that isn't going to be immediately missed. So we're back at square one, ears open and hoping for a tip-off. I thought I'd pull in Ron Hitching, who, according to the grapevine, has fallen out with Totty

Sweetman. I thought, with a bit of squeezing, he might have something to say, but he seems to have gone overboard since last night, which may or may not be significant. Anyway, it makes me want to see him even more.

'Now tell me about all your hobnobbing with the judge.'

When Patrick had finished his recital of events, D.I. Shotter said, 'Nothing we can do until Jakobson turns up. You'd better go along to the Monkes Tale this evening and keep your eyes and ears open.'

'I also want to talk to Gino Evans, sir. I gather he and Jakobson had a row last night and almost came to blows.'

D.I. Shotter nodded slowly. 'I should think a fair number of the Monkes Tale's customers feel like knocking Jakobson's head off, seeing the prices he charges.'

'Are you going to question Sweetman and Cox about today's job, sir?' Patrick asked after a silence.

'Too true, I am. Not that I shall get anywhere without a bit of leverage and that's just what I'm lacking. Leverage, Pat, a police officer's indispensable weapon.'

*   *   *

Ian Tanner and Gail had gone back to her flat in the early afternoon as soon as Judge Chaytor had adjourned the trial.

Tanner had made his feelings clear on the subject.

'We all have to pack up and go home just because the judge decides to take the afternoon off,' he observed sourly.

'Perhaps his wife's been taken ill or something.'

'More likely he wanted to go and have a game of golf.'

On arrival at the flat, Tanner tried to call Gino Evans, but could get no answer.

'What the hell's Gino doing?' he said, after a third unsuccessful attempt.

'He wouldn't know that the trial has been adjourned,'

Gail pointed out. 'I expect he'll phone you around six. Anyway, why are you anxious to talk to him?'

'There was something up with him last night. He was in the helluva state and he wouldn't say why. I want to check on how he is today, that's all.'

Gail bit her lip, but said nothing. She had become more than ever certain that Ian was holding something back from her. What she was less certain about was whether she really wanted to know the truth. There were times when it was better to let yourself be deceived.

Tanner went on ringing Gino's number at half-hourly intervals, though without response until shortly before six when Gino asnwered.

'Where the hell have you been?'

'Who is that?' Gino asked in a voice so tense as to distort it.

'Who do you think it is? Ian, of course.'

'Oh, hello. I can't stop, Ian, I've got to go out.'

'You've only just come in! I've been trying to get you the whole ruddy afternoon.'

'I'm sorry, Ian, but I can't stop.'

'Shut up and listen . . .'

'I can't, I'll call you later.'

'When?'

'I don't know . . . I've got to go.'

'What's happened, Gino? For Christ's sake, what's happened?'

But the only reply he received was the dialling tone as Gino hung up.

*   *   *

'Who pulled that job at Parsons' this morning?' Totty Sweetman's tone bristled with indignation.

Billy Cox shrugged. 'Could have been anyone.'

'Well, I want to know. And then I'll tell whoever it is to stay off my doorstep – or expect trouble.'

'Could be just a bunch of amateurs.'

'Then the sooner they learn, the better. Any moment now we're going to have the police round here asking a lot of questions and giving us a lot of aggro. All because someone does a job on our patch.'

'We have pulled jobs elsewhere, Totty,' Cox said reasonably.

'That's different. We've never deliberately invaded any-one else's territory.'

'Perhaps this lot didn't know this was our bit of living space.'

'Then they better know before they get any further fancy ideas.' He was silent for a moment. 'Where were you this morning when this job was pulled?'

'In bed with a bird.'

'Can you prove it?'

Cox nodded. 'They can't touch me. We didn't get up until eleven o'clock. The bird's sister and brother-in-law can say that. What about you?'

'I went out shopping early with Pauline. We were in the supermarket at nine.'

'That's all right then.'

'It's just what it isn't! We're still going to get a lot of aggro from the police and that's something I can do with-out. That's why I want to know who pulled the job so I can tell them to mind their step.'

'I'll see what I can find out.'

'So will I,' Sweetman said grimly. In a somewhat differ-ent tone he added, 'By the way, any news of Jakobson yet?'

Cox gave a small sardonic smile and shook his head.

'Not a dicky bird yet.'

*　　　*　　　*

150

It was just dark when Patrick brought his mini to a halt in the street in which Gino Evans lodged with an older married sister and her husband.

He was about to get out of his car when he saw Gino leave the house and hurry the other way along the street.

There was something curiously furtive about his movements so that Patrick was puzzled. He wasn't just a man going off to his local for a beer, nor yet someone in a hurry to catch a bus. It was much more the scurry of someone who was frightened but who was hoping to avoid attention.

At the farther end of the road was an area of rough ground where some old houses had been pulled down and for which Gino seemed to be making. Just before he reached the site, Patrick restarted his engine and drove slowly down the road.

Gino had disappeared on to the site while Patrick was still on his way there. As he came opposite, however, a car suddenly shot out on to the road and accelerated past Patrick with its engine protesting noisily. He was able to see Gino's tense face, his eyes peering ahead like a sea captain's into rough weather.

One of the many things to be said of a mini is its manoeuvrability and in a matter of seconds Patrick had turned and was in pursuit.

Once he had left the road in which he lived, Gino seemed to settle down to a steadier speed. Patrick kept him well in view, but made no attempt to close the gap between the two cars. Thanks to street lighting, he was able to keep a distance that wouldn't arouse the other's suspicions.

On reaching the Kingston bypass, Gino turned westward, staying on this road almost to its extremity when he made a left turn. By the time Patrick made his turn, Gino's car had disappeared and he accelerated in a sudden panic. But half a minute later he saw the tail lights ahead of him again and let out a sigh of relief. On the other hand, there was far less traffic about and great circumspection

151

was required if Gino was not to realise he was being followed. There was the further difficulty that Patrick had only a rough idea of the local geography, which certainly didn't run to a detailed knowledge of the roads.

They had been travelling for about five minutes when the car ahead made a sudden right turn. It occurred to Patrick that Gino, as least, knew exactly where he was going. He either knew the area of old or had recently reconnoitred it. Patrick had, nevertheless, become increasingly haunted by the prospect of having embarked on a pointless pursuit. Would Gino suddenly stop outside a house which proved to be that of a favourite aunt? Or, perhaps more likely, that of an innocent associate? This thought had kept on popping up in his mind since the journey had begun, but each time he'd suppressed it with the recollection of Gino's furtive air as he left home and of his tense expression as he crouched over the wheel of his car. Why should he have looked and behaved like that if he was on a perfectly normal expedition? And then there was the added factor that he had set out just as darkness had fallen. Was that fortuitous or intentional?

These thoughts were still revolving in Patrick's head when Gino's car made a sudden left turn and from the bobbing of its lights was bouncing along a bumpy track.

When Patrick arrived at the turning, he halted and turned off his lights. Almost at the same moment, he became aware that Gino's lights were no longer showing, though he could still hear the rise and fall of the engine.

He felt suddenly exhilarated, for no one drove along bumpy tracks without lights purely for fun. Also it seemed to indicate that Gino was nearing his journey's end.

Patrick could see the silhouette of a wood about two hundred yards along the track. If he followed in his car, he couldn't fail to be noticed and Gino would obviously seek to shake him off. Much depended on whether the track ran through the wood and joined a road on the far side or whether it came to a dead end. There was nothing he could do to find out and a quick decision was necessary.

A few seconds later he pulled his car across the track, so that, at least, Gino was bottled in at that end, and set off on foot armed with his powerful car torch.

There was a springy grass verge on one side of the track and beyond it a shallow ditch. Although there was no moon, the light was sufficient to pick out shapes. The land on either side of the track was common with scrub and the occasional self-sown tree sticking up out of the darkness.

As he approached closer to the wood, he was able to gauge its size. Its frontage was about eighty yards and the track looked as though it entered in the middle. He stopped a couple of times to listen. On the second occasion, he thought he could hear sounds coming from within its shelter, but he found it impossible to define them. They might even have come from nocturnal creatures about their business.

He paused a third time as he entered the wood, standing against a tree and this time straining his ears for sound.

Suddenly somewhere ahead there was the unmistakable noise of digging. Of a spade striking a stone, followed by the more muted sound of earth being shovelled.

Moving with even greater caution, he tiptoed forward, keeping to the grassy edge of the track. He had probably not gone more than fifty paces when he almost blundered into the car, which had been pulled into a small clearing on the side on which he was walking. It had already been turned round, which indicated that Gino was going to depart the same way he had come.

Crouching in front of the car, he listened intently once more. Everything seemed to have gone silent, but then he heard heavy breathing and a thud at the rear of the car, followed by the car boot being closed.

The time for stealth and caution had gone. Patrick

stood up and ran round the side of the car, switching on his torch as he did so. There was a gasp of horror and he called out, 'Don't move! Just stay where you are.'

Fixed in the beam of his torch was the terrified face of Gino Evans. At his feet lay the unmistakable shape of a body, covered over with sacking.

Keeping his torch shining on Gino, Patrick knelt down and flicked back the end of the sacking. Jeff Jakobson's face wore a slightly affronted expression as though he was being asked to endure one indignity too many.

'About to bury him, were you?' Patrick asked in a tone of pent-up excitement.

But Gino's only response was to pitch forward in a faint on top of the dead man.

CHAPTER TWELVE

After satisfying himself that Gino's faint was genuine, Patrick shone his torch around him.

About four yards away, he noticed a heap of recently turned earth and walked over to examine it. There Jakobson's grave awaited him. A closer examination showed that it had been dug some hours earlier. Clearly the sounds he had heard had been some additional spade work. Probably the sides had crumbled between its having been dug and Gino's return with the body.

He didn't know how often anyone used the track through the wood, but it seemed likely that, once filled in, the grave could have gone unnoticed for a long time. The trees were fairly close together just there and the ground was covered by bracken, which could have been successfully used to camouflage it.

Though he had never seen Gino before, he was well aware of his connection with Ian Tanner and Mick Burleigh. There had been more than a passing reference to Gino in the police file, one of the uniformed officers who compiled it having urged that consideration should be given to joining him in the prosecution on a charge of conspiracy. When in doubt suggest conspiracy, a lecturer at training school had been fond of saying.

It now seemed clear that Jakobson's death was in some way connected with Tanner's trial. But in what way? And where did Peter Chaytor fit in?

Before he had time to think of an answer to either question, there was a groan at his feet and Gino stirred.

Patrick bent down and gripped him by the upper arm. 'On your feet,' he said.

Gino rose groggily using the back of the car to steady himself.

When he was upright, Patrick stood him against the side of the car. Then, incongruous as the circumstances were, he administered the words of the caution, not that Gino seemed to be aware of the incongruity of the occasion. He closed his eyes against the beam of the torch and leaned heavily against the car as though pinned to it like a butterfly in a showcase.

Patrick had already decided that the only way to deal with the situation was to march Gino back to his car and drive to the nearest police station, leaving Gino's car and Jakobson *in situ*. Nothing much could befall either before other officers and various experts arrived on the scene. He suddenly thought of foxes and wondered whether they might look on Jeff Jakobson as a hungry refugee might regard a food parcel. He had no idea, but in case it did occur, he had better make a quick examination of Jakobson to see if there was any obvious cause of death.

'Stay there and don't move,' he said to Gino, who showed no sign of wanting to move.

Then bending down, he lifted off the pieces of sacking which covered the body.

Jakobson was fully clothed, even to still wearing his shoes. His face showed no sign of injury, but when Patrick gingerly lifted his head by the hair and shone the torch on the back, he noticed a small area of matted hair and blood. Gently lowering the head, he satisfied himself that this was the only visible injury. A quick examination of the dead man's hands showed no cuts or abrasions or what the pathologists referred to as defensive injuries.

Covering the body with sacking once more, he stood up and let out a heavy sigh. He was glad that was over. It was the first time he had examined a dead person and doing so alone in a dark wood was an eerie experience he was in no hurry to repeat.

He found that Gino had slithered to the ground so that he was now in a sitting position. His expression was dazed and he stared vacantly ahead.

Patrick helped him to his feet and took a firm grip of his arm.

'Come on, a walk'll do you good. It's also time you started talking.'

It wasn't until they had emerged from the wood that Gino said anything.

'I didn't kill him,' he muttered hoarsely.

'Who did?'

'I don't know.'

'You'll need to do better than that if you want anyone to believe you.'

'I swear I didn't kill him.'

'If you didn't kill him, why all that trouble to bury his body? You'll be telling me next that you always bury any bodies you find lying around.'

Gino let out an anguished cry. 'It was planted on me.'

'Say that again?'

'His body. I found it in the boot of my car. Somebody put it there.'

'When did you find it?' Patrick asked in a tone laden with suspicion.

'Last night. I went to put something in the boot and there it was.'

'Where was this?'

'Outside where I live. I was just going round to see Ian Tanner. I didn't know what to do. I knew no one would believe me if I told them I'd just found it there.'

'They'd have been more likely to then than twenty-four hours later when you were trying to bury it.'

'I was up half the night. I knew this spot and decided to bury it here. I dug the hole last night and covered it over.'

'And tonight you came back to finish the job?'

'Yes, I only wanted to get rid of the body. I wish now I'd gone to the police immediately.'

'I bet you do. But the hard truth is you didn't and nobody's going to believe this rubbish about the body being put into your car without your knowledge.'

'I didn't kill Jakobson,' he wailed. 'I had no reason to.'

'You had a row with him yesterday evening, didn't you?'

'Oh, my God!'

'You threatened him with violence when he told you he didn't want to see you on his premises again, didn't you?'

'I wasn't serious.'

'It sounded serious to the barman.'

Gino let out another groan of anguish.

'I swear I never meant him any harm.'

'Of course there is a difference between murder and manslaughter,' Patrick remarked in an insinuating tone. 'I mean, if, for example, you gave Jakobson a bit of a push when he was off balance and he fell backwards and cracked his head on the hearth in his office, that would be manslaughter at the most. Now, if something like that happened, the sooner the truth was known the better for everyone.'

'I never touched him, I swear I didn't. You must believe me.'

'Now let me give you the alternative scenario. You have a row with Jakobson and threaten him with violence. Later you carry out your threat and kill him and put his body in the boot of your car, intending that no one should ever find out what happened to him. Moreover, you nearly got away with it.' Patrick paused and then added, 'Personally, that's the version I find most likely.'

'No, no! I swear it's not true.'

'If that's all you can say every time, save your breath.

158

It's becoming monotonous. Anyway, what made you go to the Monkes Tale yesterday evening?'

'I was going to meet someone.'

'Who?'

'Ron Hitching.'

'Now that I find interesting. I didn't know he was a friend of yours. Why did you want to see him? Or was it the other way round?'

'Ian Tanner wanted me to see him.'

'What about?'

'Hitching used to be friendly with Totty Sweetman.'

'Well, go on!'

'Ian thought Hitching might know something.'

'About what?'

'About Mick Burleigh,' Gino said reluctantly.

'Go on!'

'That's all. I never found out. Hitching got panicky. He wouldn't talk.'

Though there were gaps in this part of Gino's story, Patrick decided not to press him further at the moment. They had reached his car and he pushed Gino into the back, not that it seemed likely he would try and escape but a two-door car reduced the temptation if he were in the back.

There was silence for a time as Patrick turned the car and drove back the way he had come.

'What's going to happen?' Gino asked in a croaking voice after they had travelled about half a mile.

'Wait and see,' Patrick said unsympathetically.

Anyway, he was busy thinking. Everything seemed to lead back to that night last autumn when Ian Tanner had taken Jakobson's car and run down Burleigh. Somehow everything that had happened subsequently was linked to that event, if only he could see the shapes more clearly. It was like one of those I.Q. tests where coloured shapes

159

made a design when correctly fitted together. The trouble at the moment was that he seemed to have too many shapes for an otherwise emerging pattern. And one of them was called Peter Chaytor.

CHAPTER THIRTEEN

A rather elderly police constable blinked in wonderment as he listened to Patrick's brief résumé of events. However, this done he locked Gino in one of the station's two cells and gave Patrick the run of his telephone.

First, he spoke to D.I. Shotter who said he'd come immediately. Next he put through a call to Judge Chaytor. He could hear the nine o'clock television news in the background when the judge lifted the receiver. It gave him a start as he'd lost all sense of time, but it seemed much more than two and a half hours since he had picked up Gino's trail.

'You say that this man Evans is a close friend of Tanner's?'

'Yes, sir. He was with him the night the car was taken. I suspect they were up to it together.'

'Is he going to be charged in connection with Jakobson's death?'

'That won't be my decision, sir.'

'No, but you must obviously have a view.'

'I would feel, sir, that the evidence needs a bit of tidying up before he's charged.'

'Like awaiting the result of the post-mortem examination?'

'Yes, sir.'

'I don't know whether it's fair to ask you this, but how, in your opinion, does this latest development affect my son?'

'I don't know, sir.' And I bloody well *don't* know, Patrick reflected as he replied. 'It'll certainly be necessary to see him again. Probably tomorrow, once we've established the cause of death and heard what else Evans may have to say. I was really only calling you, sir, as the finding of Jakobson's body might affect your decision about the continuation of the trial.'

'Yes, I realise that and I'm grateful. As I see it, Peter's involvement now seems less likely than ever. Indeed, I fail to see how he could have had anything to do with Jakobson's death. But I'm not inviting you to comment,' he added quickly. 'Incidentally, did Evans mention Peter's name at all?'

'No, sir.'

'That's a relief, too.'

'Well, I think that's all, sir.'

'Is there any reason why I shouldn't tell Peter what's happened?'

Patrick hesitated. 'That's up to you, sir,' he said eventually and felt rather pleased with this tactful piece of buck passing.

He considered that he would have to have given the judge far stronger reasons for not telling his son than he could think of, so it was really a question of bowing gracefully to the inevitable.

Nevertheless, he wished he could be a fly on the wall when the news was broken to Peter Chaytor. If he had known what his reaction would be, he'd have wished it even more.

It was one of pop-eyed stupefaction, which left even his father puzzled and disturbed.

*   *   *

Patrick decided that he had time to phone Jennie in the lull before the storm. Once Detective Inspector Shotter, accompanied possibly by more senior brass, arrived, there would certainly be no opportunity to do so.

'Hello, Mrs King, it's me, Patrick,' he said when he heard Jennie's mother's voice on the line.

'Good evening, Pat,' she said in a tone in which he thought he detected a faint note of embarrassment. 'Jennie was expecting you to ring earlier.'

'I would have done, but I was out on a job and couldn't get to a telephone. Is she there now?'

'She's upstairs washing her hair.'

'Can I speak to her?'

'I'll go and find out.'

It was at least a couple of minutes before the telephone came to life again.

'If you don't mind waiting, she'll be down in a few minutes,' Mrs King said on her return. In a lowered voice she added, 'I think I should warn you, Pat, she's a bit upset.'

'What's happened?'

'She's upset that you've not called earlier.'

'I couldn't. I can explain that to her.'

'Well, I thought I'd just warn you. I can hear her coming now.'

Patrick heard the receiver changing hands and then Jennie's voice came down the line, cool and distant.

'Yes?'

'I'm terribly sorry I didn't ring earlier, Jennie, but I was following someone in my car and it turned out to be quite a chase.'

'I see.'

'This chap had a dead body in his car.'

'Oh.'

'He was going to bury it in a wood if I hadn't arrived on the scene.'

'Very dramatic, I'm sure.'

'I know you're cross with me, but I really am terribly sorry.'

'If that's all, I must go. My hair's all wet.'

'Oh, Jennie, please don't sound so stiff and angry!'

'I'm not angry,' she said in the same implacable tone. 'Why should I be angry? After all there's nothing new in what you've done. It's always happening.'

'What can I do to make you forgive me?'

'Why should you worry whether I forgive you? You're obviously having a very exciting time. I mean, dead bodies being buried in woods, you must be right in your element. Anyway, what is there to forgive? I've always realised your job came first and I only get the odd hour that's left over.'

'Jennie, please! You know that's not so. I love you. I hate having hurt you like this.'

'I'm afraid I can't talk any longer, I must go and dry my hair.'

'When am I going to see you?'

She gave a short, mirthless laugh. 'Fancy *you* asking *me* that!'

'Can we go out tomorrow evening?' he asked desperately.

'How do you know you won't be busy preventing more bodies being buried in woods?'

'May I call you?'

'I can hardly stop you. I can't hang on any longer, so I'll say good night.'

Patrick stared forlornly at the receiver in his hand. He was about to replace it when a voice brought it to life again.

'Are you still there, Pat?' Mrs King asked.

'Yes. Jennie's very upset with me, isn't she?'

'I did warn you.'

'Put in a good word for me, Mrs King?'

'There's nothing much I can do, Pat. I like you, you know that, but this is something you and Jennie must sort out for yourselves. I've always been staunchly pro-police, but I can now see the snags of being married to a policeman. You have to be wedded to his career as well.'

Patrick sighed. 'And yet policemen need wives as much as anyone else.'

Mrs King laughed lightly. 'I expect Jennie will feel differently tomorrow, though don't bank on it. But give her a call and take her out if you can. That'll be a start to mending your fences. I'd better go. I hear her calling me. I usually help her set her hair.'

Patrick thought it more likely that she merely wanted her mother to stop talking to him.

'Hell!' he said aloud, with a wealth of feeling.

It was half past one before he got to bed that night. After D.I. Shotter's arrival at the station, they had gone to the wood and examined the scene by the light of mobile lamps. Photographs had been taken and eventually Jeff Jakobson's body had been taken away to the mortuary to await the attention of the pathologist. A uniformed constable was given the job of driving Gino's car back to the station where its boot could be examined at leisure in the morning by an expert from the Metropolitan Police Laboratory. Finally, the area was cordoned off and tarpaulins were erected above ground level to preserve the scene.

As Patrick accompanied D.I. Shotter back to their own station, Shotter said, 'I suppose we'd better tackle Evans as soon as we return, though I doubt whether we'll get any more out of him than what he's already told you. Once the cause of death has been established, we'll probably have enough to justify a charge, but until then and the result of the lab tests, we'll just have to persuade him to be our guest, helping us with our enquiries, as the newspapers always have it.'

It was getting on for midnight when Gino was fetched from his cell and D.I. Shotter introduced himself.

'Just a few questions before you have your shut-eye. You're not too tired, are you?'

Gino shook his head as though already in a dream. 'I've

told him everything I know,' he muttered, nodding in Patrick's direction.

'You realise you're in a fix, don't you? Trying to bury bodies in woods is a serious matter. Could hardly be more serious.'

'I didn't kill him.'

'Saying that won't help you very much. It's like the lad with jam all over his face, saying he's been nowhere near the larder. And by God, you've got an awful lot of jam on your face!' Gino shook his head again, though whether as a gesture of denial or of disbelief wasn't clear. 'If you didn't kill Jakobson, how did the body get into your car?'

'I don't know.'

'Who put it there?'

'I tell you I don't know.'

'Who was your accomplice.'

'I didn't have an accomplice.'

'Did it all on your own, did you?'

'I didn't do anything.'

'Didn't do anything! You were trying to bury a body in the utmost secrecy. Bury it so that it would never be found. You call that doing nothing?'

'I was frightened.'

'What of?'

'I didn't think the police would believe me if I told them I'd just found it in the boot.'

'So you decided to make matters worse? Is that what you're asking me to believe?'

'I've told you,' Gino wailed.

'Supposing you *are* telling the truth – and it's a very big *supposing* – why should anyone want to put Jakobson's body into *your* car?'

'I don't know,' he said in a frightened whisper.

'Do you have any enemies?'

'No.'

'You don't expect me to believe that, do you? You've

166

been using the Monkes Tale for quite a long time, haven't you?'

'Yes, but not recently. After what happened over the car, Jeff didn't want to see us there too much.'

'You know Totty Sweetman, of course?'

'I've seen him there,' Gino replied with sudden wariness.

'Friend of yours, is he?'

'No.'

'An enemy, then?'

'No, just someone I've seen.'

'What about Billy Cox?'

'Same.'

'You and Tanner and Burleigh used to fancy yourselves quite a bit, didn't you?'

'How do you mean?'

'I picked up something on the grapevine once which said you were thinking of pulling a job together. It was only junior league stuff, but you had big ideas, it was said.'

Gino licked his lips. 'Somebody didn't know what they were talking about.'

'Ever do any jobs for Sweetman?'

'Never.' After a pause he added belatedly, 'Never done any jobs at all.'

D.I. Shotter yawned. 'Well, my advice to you, my lad, is to have a good hard think about your position. You're in a mess and the sort of tales you've been telling us this evening aren't going to get you out of it. We'll be having another chat tomorrow, by which time you'd better have thought of something more sensible to say. I know you probably think we're a gullible lot in the police, but there's a limit to what even we'll swallow.'

Patrick took Gino Evans back to his cell and rejoined D.I. Shotter out in the car park.

'God, I'm tired!' Shotter said.

'Any further developments on the Parsons job, sir?'

'Not yet, but we'll pick up a scent sooner or later. Someone'll let drop a word which'll filter back to us. I had Sweetman and Cox along at the station just before you called this evening.'

'Do you still think they were involved?'

'I doubt it now. Totty Sweetman was all injured innocence when he wasn't waxing indignant. Billy Cox was just his dour self. But there doesn't seem to be anything against either of them.'

'Still no sign of Hitching?'

'I've rather lost interest in him now. If Sweetman didn't have anything to do with the job at Parsons, there's nothing I want to talk about with Ron Hitching.'

Patrick nodded. He, on the other hand, had decided he would definitely like to have a word with Hitching. He wondered, too, why he had chosen this particular moment to go overboard.

In fact, Hitching was uppermost in his thoughts as he set his alarm for seven o'clock and a couple of minutes later fell fast asleep.

CHAPTER FOURTEEN

News of the discovery of Jakobson's body spread quickly at the Old Bailey the next morning. One or two newspapers had carried a short item about police finding a body in a wood but no names were mentioned.

Ian Tanner heard it from his solicitor's clerk who had happened to bump into Patrick as he was arriving at court.

'No wonder Gino was in a state!' Tanner said, on relaying the news to Gail as they waited outside the court-room.

'Does that mean he killed Jakobson?' Gail asked.

'Can't think what he was otherwise doing with the body in his car.'

'But why should he have killed him?'

'Search me, girl! He must have been getting up to something or other.'

'You don't think it's connected with . . . with your case?'

Tanner's expression changed abruptly, a familiar scowling frown settling over his features.

'How could it be?'

'Gino may have gone to see Jakobson about the case.'

'I never asked him to.'

'But he was trying to find out about Mick Burleigh, why he was in Waterworks Lane.'

'Jakobson wouldn't know. He was in Spain at the time. I don't know what you're getting at, Gail.'

Gail sighed heavily. 'I'm not getting at anything. I'm as much in the dark about what happened that night as I've always been. I'm in the dark because I know you haven't told me everything. You and Gino have both kept things back from me. You've wanted my help, but you haven't ever been ready to trust me. That's true, isn't it, Ian?'

Tanner looked at her with a mixture of horror and dismay. 'This is a fine time to start rocking the boat, just as you're about to give evidence for me.'

'Oh, I'll give evidence for you all right. Don't worry, I won't let you down, but it's about time you realised how I've felt about your deceiving me.'

'I've never deceived you,' he said vehemently. 'Honest, I haven't.'

'Well, you've certainly not told me the truth.'

'How can you say that?'

'Because you've never told me the real reason you took the car. I don't believe it was simply for a joy-ride.'

Tanner gave a small squirm of impatience.

'Why do you think I took it then?' he asked belligerently.

'I don't know because you've never told me.'

He hadn't told her because he feared her reaction. It was not that she thought he was an angel, but rather that she shouldn't have certain of his activities thrust right under her nose. As long as she didn't know too much, she didn't mind what he got up to. Or so he had believed until now when she was reproaching him for not having told her everything. The trouble was that it had become so protracted. It was six months since he had taken Jakobson's car that dark autumn night and here they were the following spring re-enacting events in front of the distorting mirror of a court-room.

He decided there was only one thing to do in the circumstances, namely put on his piteous small boy look. Before, however, it had had time to take effect on Gail's mothering instinct, Andrew Batchford had joined them.

'I gather you've heard about Jakobson's death?' he said.

170

They both nodded. 'It doesn't make any difference to the trial, does it?' Tanner asked.

'Not unless it's suggested that he was killed because of the evidence he gave.'

'That'd be as good as saying that I had something to do with his death.'

'Which of course you didn't.'

'Right.'

'Nevertheless, I think I'll just have a word with prosecuting counsel before we get going.'

Andrew Batchford pushed his way through the swing doors into court. Mr Ridge was already in his seat, leaning back with a complacent air as though he had just bought the building.

'Oh, good morning, Batchford,' he said, complacence giving way to an expression of self-importance. 'You've heard about my witness Jakobson's death?'

'I have.'

'You're not going to suggest it invalidates the evidence he gave?'

'Can I?' Andrew Batchford asked in a tone of faint irony.

'I'd certainly argue that his evidence stands.'

'You can save your breath. Of course it does.'

'Oh, I'm glad you agree.'

'It'll be in the papers by this evening and the jury'll know about it then if they haven't heard before, which they probably will have done. I have no doubt that the judge will mention it in his summing-up when he deals with Jakobson's evidence, but I suggest that neither the prosecution nor the defence try and make anything of it.'

'Oh, I quite agree,' Mr Ridge said without hesitation.

Andrew Batchford looked at him doubtfully. He hoped he really had secured his opponent's agreement, but you could never be absolutely sure with someone as inex-

171

perienced and as stupid as Bruce Ridge. He blundered into things like one of those large, noisy may-bugs.

'I don't know where the officer is,' he went on. 'He should be here by now.' He gave a sharp laugh. 'They're never here when you need them.'

In fact, Patrick was at that moment in the judge's room. He had not been surprised to be summoned to Judge Chaytor's presence before the court sat.

'So you can't really add anything to what you told me on the telephone last night?' Matthew Chaytor observed after Patrick had confirmed the position regarding Gino Evans.

'No, sir.'

'Evans' story sounds totally implausible. But supposing it were true, what offence has he committed?' Patrick blinked and the judge smiled. 'I suppose you think if anyone should know, it ought to be a judge. I expect there's some such offence as obstructing a burial under one of those Victorian Acts of Parliament. However, I imagine you'll probably also get him as an accessory after the fact. If he knew Jakobson had been killed and he agreed to dispose of the body, he'd certainly be an accessory to the principal crime.' He gave Patrick another quick smile. 'When I was at the bar, I never ceased to be impressed by the ingenuity shown by police officers in finding charges to cover the most bizarre circumstances. Well, I suppose you want to get into court, so I mustn't keep you.' He glanced at his watch. 'I'll be sitting in about fifteen minutes' time.'

Patrick turned to go and then paused. He felt that, having served the judge's purpose, he was entitled to ask a few questions himself.

'Did you tell your son, sir, about the discovery of Jakobson's body?'

'Yes, I thought it was only fair to do so.' He shifted his gaze to the window and Patrick had the impression

172

that he was deliberately avoiding looking at him. 'Naturally, he was very relieved.'

'Did he say anything?'

'No.'

'Did he not show any reaction at all?'

'I've told you, he was relieved,' the judge said a trifle sharply.

'I hope you didn't mind my asking, sir?'

'Of course not,' the judge replied with a quick change to affability.

But he had minded, Patrick reflected. He definitely hadn't liked being quizzed about his son's reaction to the news.

'I'll still need to see him again.'

'I reminded him of that after you called last night. Now, if you'll excuse me, Bramley . . .'

As Patrick left the judge's room, an idea began to form in his head as to what might have happened on the evening of Jakobson's death. It involved a curious sequence of events, though, for the life of him, he was quite unable to ascribe them any motive. And where were you without a motive?

*　　　*　　　*

There had been times over the past two days when Gail felt that her whole life had been spent in waiting to give evidence.

When her name was first called in the corridor outside the court, she heard it clearly enough but completely failed to react. The usher called it a second time and was turning to go back into court when she sprang up.

'You Miss Norbet?' he asked suspiciously, having seen her sitting there and making no attempt to move.

'Yes, I'm sorry, I was dreaming.'

173

'Better not dream when you're in the witness-box, my dear,' he remarked.

Gail followed him through the glass-panelled doors into court. When she reached the witness box she stared around her in a bemused manner. It was the first time she had ever been in a real live court-room and it was totally different from being a fly on the wall in a television court-room.

Ian was staring at her with a worried frown. He wasn't physically very far from her, but he managed to look infinitely remote. She felt a pang seeing him sitting in the dock with two prison officers nearby as though he was a dangerous criminal.

She took the oath in a trancelike state and then fixed her gaze on the judge because he had a comfortable, secure air about him in all this strangeness.

She heard her name being spoken and turned her head to see Andrew Batchford addressing her. She hadn't noticed him when she first came into court, he being lost in a sea of bewigged heads. She wondered who all the others were and was later to learn that they were mostly young barristers who wandered from court to court watching and learning.

'Is your name Gail Norbet?'

'Yes, sir,' she said in a timid whisper.

'You'll have to speak louder than that, Miss Norbet. It's most important that all of us, and particularly the jury, hear your evidence. Now, I want to ask you some questions about the evening of the accident. You know to what I'm referring?'

'Yes.'

'When did you first know about the accident?'

'When Ian arrived.'

'Ian is the defendant?'

'Yes.'

'And where did he arrive?'

'At my flat.'

174

'What time was it?'

'Between eleven and half past.'

'How did he appear to you?'

'He seemed terribly shocked.'

'Was he able to tell you what had happened?'

'Not really.' Gail bit her lip and went on in a voice that trembled, 'It seemed to have affected his memory.'

'In what way?'

'He couldn't remember what had happened.'

'But he told you he'd been involved in an accident?'

'Yes.'

'What else did he tell you at the time?'

'I don't think he said anything else. Bits came back to him later.' She paused and frowned as if trying to recall something learnt by heart. 'He did say that someone had run out in front of the car and that he couldn't avoid him. It was what happened afterwards he couldn't remember.'

Gail became aware of the judge looking at her over the top of his spectacles and swallowed nervously.

'Did he seem to know who had run out in front of the car?'

'No. We only heard later that it was Mick Burleigh.'

'What was Tanner's reaction when he learnt that?'

'He was terribly upset. He just couldn't understand what had happened.'

'Do you have any doubt, Miss Norbet, that his state of shock when he arrived at your flat was genuine?'

'None.'

'Thank you. I have no further questions to ask.'

Mr Ridge rose to his feet and threw the witness the sort of look that warned her to expect thunderbolts.

'Did you immediately send for the doctor?'

'I beg your pardon?'

'I'm asking if you sent for the doctor to attend to the defendant?'

175

'No.'

'Why not?'

'It wasn't necessary.'

'Not necessary? Here he was in this terrible state of shock and you say it wasn't necessary?'

'No ... yes ... I mean ...'

'*What* do you mean?'

There is nothing more agonising for counsel than to watch one of his witnesses crumbling before his eyes – and Andrew Batchford now had that experience. That it should be Bruce Ridge who was bringing it about did nothing to alleviate his suffering. He didn't even regard her evidence as particularly useful, but Tanner had insisted that she be called and so he'd agreed, thinking that no harm, even if no actual good, would ensue. Now it was unlikely that the jury would believe this story of shock and mild amnesia and that, in turn, would cast doubt on the rest of Tanner's evidence. Andrew Batchford felt especially let down as he had regarded Gail as being a sensible sort of girl. That she was extremely nervous was all too apparent, but why if she had come along to tell the truth? Ah well, he could only do his best and it certainly wasn't the first time that counsel's efforts had been undermined by those they were serving.

Gail clutched the edge of the witness-box. Her mind had gone blank and she felt that everyone was looking at her. If she had known it was going to be like this, she would never have come near the court. She had only wanted to help Ian and here she was faltering with everyone staring at her like vultures waiting to pick her bones.

'Would you like to sit down, Miss Norbet?' the judge asked in a not unkindly voice.

'Yes, please, sir.'

'Give the witness a glass of water,' he added to the usher.

'How long have you known the defendant?' Mr Ridge asked.

176

'Just over a year.'

'Are you very fond of him?'

'Yes.'

'You don't sound very certain.'

'I like him very much.'

'Enough to help him when he's in trouble?'

'Yes.'

'Like giving evidence for him?'

'Yes.'

'And supporting everything he has said?'

'It's true what I've said.'

'I don't think I need ask this witness any further questions, my lord,' Mr Ridge said, casting the jury a meaningful glance.

Andrew Batchford indicated that he didn't wish to re-examine and Gail left the witness-box with a feeling of intense relief. She looked toward Ian, but his eyes were fixed on the dock floor and it seemed that he was deliberately avoiding meeting her gaze.

An usher came across and passed Patrick a piece of folded paper. It was a telephone message asking him to call D.I. Shotter as soon as he was able.

He tiptoed out of court and went up to the police room where he dialled the number.

'I thought you'd like to know the result of the post mortem on Jeff Jakobson. He died of natural causes, a massive heart attack.'

Patrick let out a gasp. 'What about the injury to his head, sir?'

'Only superficial. Bled a lot, but nothing else. No underlying fractures.'

'What does the pathologist think happened then?'

'That he was struck down by a sudden coronary and hit his head on the hearth when he fell.'

'So what are we going to do about Evans, sir?'

'Search the books for a charge. You're not allowed to

177

bury bodies privately even if they did die from natural causes.'

'It is possible, sir, that he had the heart attack because someone pushed him or scared him?'

'I'd say it was more than possible, Pat. That's just what we're going to find out.'

CHAPTER FIFTEEN

Ron Hitching knew he had been right to disappear as soon as he phoned his place of work and learnt that some-one had been enquiring after him. He felt doubly right when he rang the house in which he lodged and was told that someone had been round there asking for him. In each case it was clear from the answers he received that the someone was Billy Cox.

He had moved outside the area and taken a room in a small terraced house in Wandsworth, where he had paid for two weeks in advance. He was hoping that by then he would be able to return to his old lodging. Moreover, he had no wish to change his job. He had told the foreman that he was sick and hoped to be back in a few days, which was a sufficiently elastic arrangement for him to stay away a bit longer if necessary.

He wasn't bright enough to realise that once you fell foul of Totty Sweetman, the wisest course was to take yourself well away. At least, it was not so much a lack of brightness as a streak of naivety which blunted his percep-tion.

He had never been one of Totty Sweetman's most com-mitted supporters and, like the guests summoned to the biblical wedding feast, had been making excuses for not becoming involved in this or that criminal enterprise some time before his actual defection. Though he had been careful not to give the impression of any move as dramatic as a defection. It had been more like a slow withdrawal.

As Tricia Burleigh's boy-friend at the time, he had been shocked by her brother's death. Not only shocked but conscience-stricken, for if there was anyone to be cast in the role of Judas, it was he.

At lunchtime he went out to drink a lonely pint of beer in a strange pub full of unfamiliar faces. Outside the pub he bought a midday paper, primarily to pick a few winners as he proposed spending the afternoon in a betting shop.

Before turning to the racing pages, he scanned the news items on the front of the paper. It was there on the front page that he read of Jeff Jakobson's death and of the discovery of his body beside an open grave in a Surrey wood. A young man, it was reported, was helping the police with their enquiries and a charge was likely to be preferred before the day was over.

Hitching left his beer untouched as he read and re-read the short paragraph. Although, as part of his endeavour to steer clear of Sweetman, he had ceased going to the Monkes Tale, he still had an interest in what went on there. He knew, for example, that Totty Sweetman had once persuaded Jakobson to hide some stolen jewellery for him and that this had led to ructions when Jakobson demanded a higher percentage of the proceeds than Sweetman thought reasonable. However, their relationship had been patched up and had resulted in an uneasy truce. He also knew that Jakobson acquired much of his booze at lower than cut prices from sources about which one didn't enquire too closely. In a word he knew that Jeff Jakobson was an expert fiddler.

It was in a heavily reflective mood that he downed his pint and stared into his empty glass, as he tried to decide on his best course of action. The trouble was that there were almost too many options open to him.

Of course, it might have been simpler if he had realised that he held a key to the central mystery. *He* happened to know what Mick Burleigh was doing in Waterworks Lane that night.

180

But, as is often the case, familiarity with a situation deprives a person of the ability to recognise its significance and all Ron Hitching could think of was that his own life was somehow in danger.

CHAPTER SIXTEEN

Patrick felt almost blasé as he made his way 'back-stage' to the judge's room as soon as the court adjourned at lunchtime. It had become a well-worn path during the past two days and he no longer required an usher to conduct him.

Judge Chaytor waved him to a chair. 'I observed your getting a message and leaving court,' he said with a faint self-deprecatory smile. 'Has there been a further development?'

'Yes, sir, the post mortem on Jakobson showed that he died of a heart attack. The injury to the back of his head was caused when he collapsed on the floor, but didn't play any part in his death.'

'Well, well,' the judge said in a thoughtful tone. 'He died of a coronary, did he?'

'Yes,' Patrick said and waited for the judge to go on.

'Do you still wish to interview Peter again?'

'I'd like to as soon as possible, just to clear up one or two stray ends.'

'If you like, I'll call my home now and perhaps you could go along this afternoon. Now that we're coming on to speeches, I don't suppose there's anything to keep you in court.'

'That would suit me fine, sir.'

'I can't believe you will miss much by not hearing prosecuting counsel's address to the jury. Nor would I expect my summing-up to give you much inspiration. Not that I shall get very far with it today, if I begin at all.' He reached for the telephone and gave the girl his home number. 'As you'll realise, you've lifted a great load off my mind. It's an enormous relief to know that Peter's in the clear over this whole miserable business.' Patrick said nothing but couldn't help wondering why, if he was so much in the clear, he had taken to his heels and fled home in such a panic. 'I suppose all I have to worry about now is the possible publicity. It would be nice to think that his name won't be dragged in to it. Nice, but naive, I fear. "Judge's son knew secret grave victim" will prove an irresistible headline for some papers.' He sighed. 'That'll be our problem if and when it arises.' The telephone on his desk gave a mild tinkle and he lifted the receiver. 'Philippa? It's Matt. I've just heard that the man Jakobson died of a heart attack . . . yes, of natural causes . . . Mr Bramley, the officer who saw Peter yesterday, would like to come and talk to him this afternoon . . . no, just to clear up one or two points. After all, Peter was the last known person to see Jakobson alive . . . He hasn't gone out has he? . . . Good! Well tell him to expect Mr Bramley early this afternoon . . . no, he'll be coming alone. I can't get away. I'll be home the usual time. Good-bye dear.'

Patrick could never hear himself calling Jennie 'dear'. It was more like a flick of cold water than a term of affection. Perhaps when you've been married for two decades and more, even endearments were apt to become as functional as punctuation marks. With a small stab of conscience, he realised that it was the first time Jennie had come into his thoughts since she had given him such a chilly reception on the telephone. He pulled a slight face of wry remorse, while the judge was scribbling something down on a slip of paper.

'Just reminding myself of something,' Judge Chaytor said, looking up. 'As you'll have gathered, it's all right to go this afternoon. Peter was only just getting up when I called. Personally, I think it's a bad thing to let him lie in bed half the day, but my wife deludes herself into thinking he needs the rest. Perhaps you will let me know how the interview goes. Ring me here at the Old Bailey after the court rises.' Apparently feeling that some explanation was required for the request, he added drily, 'Peter and I don't communicate very well, so unless you tell me what transpires, I'm unlikely to learn.'

It was just after half past two when Patrick drew up outside the Chaytors' house in Hampstead.

Mrs Chaytor opened the front door to let him in.

'I'm afraid I didn't have an opportunity to talk to you when you were here yesterday,' she said as they stood in the hall. 'I know it's a cliché, but Peter's a very mixed-up boy. Lawyers, and my husband is no exception, are not noted for their sympathy toward people with psychiatric difficulties. They feel the need to rationalise everything and stand everyone beside that laughable figure, the reasonable man. As if *he* had ever existed!'

'I can assure you, Mrs Chaytor, that your husband showed considerable understanding of Peter's position.'

'Made a good plea in mitigation, did he?' she remarked with a funny little smile. 'Please don't misunderstand me, I'm not a besotted mum who won't believe her son can do any wrong, but Peter has had, and does have, his problems and I'm just asking that he should be judged against himself and not against the non-existent reasonable man.

Patrick felt puzzled. 'I'm not clear why you're saying this to me, Mrs Chaytor. I mean, I heard your husband tell you on the phone that Jakobson had died of natural causes. That means no one can be charged in relation to his death.'

Philippa Chaytor stared at him with a searching expression for a full minute before speaking. 'Something brought Peter home in a state of panic, if not of shock. I'm sure that hasn't escaped your notice, Mr Bramley, as you're obviously an intelligent and alert young man. All I'm asking is that you bear in mind that someone like Peter can be sent into a panic by something that would leave the fictitious

185

reasonable man unmoved. That's all.' She moved toward the top of the stairs which led down to the kitchen. 'Peter, Mr Bramley's on his way down,' she called out and stood aside for Patrick to pass.

Peter Chaytor was sitting, as before, with a newspaper spread out on the table before him. At his right elbow was a bowl of cereal into which he dipped a spoon without taking his attention off the paper. As Patrick watched, he brought the spoon slowly across to his mouth while it dripped milk en route.

It was not until Patrick had sat down opposite him that he glanced up from the newspaper. He said nothing, but immediately began fiddling with his beard with the hand that wasn't holding a spoon.

'You've heard about the discovery of Jakobson's body?' Patrick said. Peter Chaytor nodded warily. 'And that he died of a heart attack?' Another nod. 'As far as we know, you were still the last person to see him alive. What position did you say he was in when you left his office?'

Peter Chaytor blinked uncertainly while he twisted two strands of beard round a finger. It's a wonder he hasn't pulled it right off, Patrick reflected as he waited for a reply.

'I think he was standing beside his desk.'

'So that if he fell backwards, he would hit his head against the edge of the brick hearth?'

'Yes.'

'I see,' Patrick said, giving him a thoughtful gaze. 'Was that the position he was in when you hit him?'

Peter Chaytor gave a small gasp and actually wrenched a hair from his chin.

'That's what happened, Peter, isn't it? You had a row, you hit him or gave him a push and he fell back and hit his head. You thought you'd killed him, even though you'd never intended that, and you fled. What you didn't know was that, in his excitable state following your row, Jakobson had a sudden massive coronary thrombosis which

186

felled him. The pathologist says he might have dropped dead at any moment given the condition of his arteries. Isn't that what happened?'

Peter Chaytor shook his head in a bemused way. 'I've told you the truth.'

'You said just now,' Patrick went on in a tone of patient firmness, 'that Jakobson was standing beside his desk when you last saw him. Yesterday when I asked you the same question you told me he was sitting down when you left his office. They can't both be true. Personally, I believe he was standing up as you said just now.' Patrick took a deep breath. 'Look, Peter, I can't make any promises, but if it happened as I think, you may well not have committed any offence. If, as I suspect, you did give Jakobson a blow or a push, it was not sufficient to raise any injury. If you had struck him hard enough, the pathologist would almost certainly have found a bruise or a mark of some sort.' He paused. 'Now that I've come clean with you, why don't you do the same with me?'

For a time Peter Chaytor stared mesmerised at his spoon as he waved it slowly to and fro like a metronome. Then he returned it to the bowl of half-eaten cereal which he pushed away from him. Abruptly, in a totally unemotional voice, he began talking.

'We had a row. It'd been boiling up over several days about this other matter . . .'

'The whisky and your speeding?'

Chaytor nodded. 'He'd worked himself up into a temper and tried to make out I'd behaved like a tiresome child and given him a lot of trouble with the police. He hinted that he might decide to sell me down the river, even though all I'd done was follow his instructions. He said he'd told me to remove certain labels from the cases of whisky, but he never had. I was worried about what might happen, but he seemed to take a sadistic pleasure in keeping me dangling over how he was going to handle the matter. As

I say, we did have a row that night because he wanted to have one. He wanted an excuse to belittle me and make me squirm. In the end, I lost my temper. He thought I was going to attack him and he became tremendously agitated and shouted even more at me. His face was a horrible livid. I just gave him a violent push and he seemed to topple backwards. He let out one terrible gasp when he was on the floor and then he lay quite still. I bent over him, but his breathing had ceased and then I saw the blood on the hearth. I thought I'd killed him even though I had never intended to. But I knew it would be manslaughter even so. I've never been so frightened in all my life. I just ran. My one idea was to put distance between myself and the Monkes Tale.'

'You left him lying dead on the floor?'

'Yes.'

'Hmm!' Patrick was thoughtful for a moment. 'Do you know Gino Evans?'

'Tanner's friend?'

'Yes.'

'No. He hasn't been coming to the Monkes Tale since I've been there.'

'He was there on the night of Jakobson's death. Did you happen to see him?'

'No.'

'What was Jakobson's relationship with Totty Sweetman?'

'I think he was frightened of Sweetman.'

'But was Jakobson involved in any of Sweetman's crookery?'

'I wouldn't know. He could have been, but he never used to talk about Sweetman when I was around. Jeff Jakobson was a fairly devious sort of person and he knew how to look after number one.'

'Are you ready to sign a statement setting out what you've told me?'

'Do I have to?'

'In theory no, in practice it would be very desirable.'

'From whose point of view?'

'Mine,' Patrick said with a grin.

'Do you mean a statement under caution?'

'No, I mean a witness statement.'

'What about the other matter, the speeding and whisky affair?'

'That's not my concern. Other officers from another station are investigating it. You'll be told the decision when you report in accordance with the terms of your bail.'

It took Patrick three quarters of an hour to record Peter Chaytor's statement, in the course of which time Mrs Chaytor suddenly appeared in the kitchen doorway.

'Is everything all right?' she asked in an anxious voice.

'Yes, mother,' her son replied. 'I'm just making a statement.'

She shot Patrick a reproachful look but, after several seconds of obvious indecision, retired upstairs again.

Patrick was putting the statement away in his briefcase when Peter Chaytor said, 'Are you going to tell my father what I've said?'

'It'd be much better if you told him.'

Peter made a face, 'He's not an easy person to talk to. We've never hit it off. He'll be glad when I've gone again.'

'You may be underestimating his feeling for you.'

'No, I'm not. I'm an embarrassing sort of son for a judge to have.' His face broke into a smile for the first time since Patrick had met him. It was a funny twisted smile. 'And he's an embarrassing father for someone who lives like me.'

'Why not tell your mother then?'

'Perhaps.'

'Don't you wish to relieve her anxiety?'

'I don't want either of my parents to regard me as the

189

prodigal son returned. Because I haven't returned in that sense.'

There was a note of egotism in his tone which stung Patrick to reply.

'You came running here quickly enough when you were in trouble.'

Peter Chaytor gave a dismissive shrug and affected sudden interest in the newspaper spread out in front of him.

Patrick got up and walked across to the door. He wondered whether to add that in his view Peter Chaytor wasn't so much mixed up as spoilt. But what was the point? It wasn't any of his business and what mattered was that he had a statement which, he was satisfied, represented the truth as far as it went.

Mrs Chaytor was hovering at the head of the stairs and looked questioningly at Patrick as he came up.

'I said I'd phone your husband, Mrs Chaytor, but he'll still be in court. Perhaps you'll tell him that I don't expect to have to see Peter again. He's made a statement covering his knowledge of the matter and that's the end of it. There's no evidence in my view to justify any charge against him in relation to Jakobson's death or disappearance, nor has he said anything which could bear on the case your husband is trying.'

As he finished speaking, he walked quickly toward the front door in order to forestall any questions Mrs Chaytor might have in mind. He bade her a hurried farewell and departed.

It was only when he was driving away he reflected that, for a Temporary Detective Constable, he had certainly taken a great deal on his own shoulders. But like most young men, he found that decisions came easily and he had no qualms about the way he had handled the interview.

Indeed, he suddenly realised how much he had enjoyed and relished the last two days.

190

CHAPTER SEVENTEEN

With a jerk of his head, Sweetman motioned to Billy Cox to follow him out of the kitchen where Pauline Sweetman had begun cooking the evening meal.

They went into the front room where Sweetman quietly closed the door.

'I've been thinking,' he said in a grim tone. 'We made a bad mistake the other evening, letting Ron get out of our sights. It'd have been better if we'd arranged a little accident there and then. Now, he's gone overboard and can make all sorts of trouble.'

'You think he'll dare, Totty?'

'Scared men are dangerous men.'

'Anyway, little accidents take a bit of time to arrange and we didn't have any time that evening. We didn't know he was going to be there meeting Evans. It was just luck we spotted them.'

'If I hadn't bumped into Evans in the car park, we'd never have known anything.'

'Wonder which of 'em had got in touch with the other?'

'And why?'

'And why?' Billy Cox echoed.

'We'd have had answers to those questions if we hadn't mucked our chance. Instead of putting the frighteners on Ron we ought to have grabbed him while we could.'

'It'd have needed organising and I still say we didn't have the time.'

'Maybe, but we've got to find him now. I don't trust Ron any more and we must get him quickly. Get him before he walks into some cop-shop.'

'He'd never do that, Totty.'

'He might. Ron's always been a bit soft at the centre. But . . .' Sweetman paused significantly, 'I wouldn't be surprised if the law doesn't start looking for him. And if they find him, he could be easier to crack than a soft-boiled egg.'

'O.K., so we find him.'

'And remove him.'

'What do you suggest?'

'Something unmessy. Send him to the bottom of the river is as good a way as any.'

Billy Cox nodded. 'And easy, too.'

'The whole bloody affair should have taught us a lesson,' Sweetman said angrily. 'Not to try and be too bloody clever. If you can take a hammer to the job, don't use a feather duster.'

Billy Cox laughed. 'Come off it, Totty. We've not done too badly.'

'We've not done too well, either.'

'We've taught lessons where lessons needed to be taught.'

'We've given ourselves a lot of unnecessary aggro, too. And now we've got to find Ron before he can add to the load.'

'I reckon I'll be on to him within twenty-four hours.'

'You haven't got any longer. And by now he'll know we're looking for him.'

'Don't worry, Totty. I'll find him. Ron's not too clever at covering his tracks. And when I find him, I'll catch him as easy as a flea on the back of a hairless dog.'

*　　　*　　　*

When Patrick arrived back at the station, he learnt that D.I. Shotter had gone off in a hurry to a station in Y Division in North London to interview someone detained there, who might know something about the robbery at Parsons, the jewellers.

Before leaving, he had given instructions that Gino Evans was to be released on bail under Section 38 of the Magistrates Court Act 1952 which meant that unless he received contrary notice he had to report to the police station on a specified date when he would either be charged or told that no charge was forthcoming. It was the procedure under which Peter Chaytor had been released and which gave the police time to scratch around for evidence and, in Gino Evans' case, also to scratch their own and lawyers' heads as to what offence he had actually committed.

The necessary documentation had not been completed by the time Patrick returned so that Gino was still at the station. Patrick met him as he was leaving the general office, an anxious and subdued looking figure.

'You're a lucky chap, aren't you?' he remarked agreeably.

'I don't know where the luck comes in,' Gino replied in a dispirited tone.

'You never expected last night that you'd be walking out of the police station free this afternoon, did you?'

'I was framed.'

'Who by?'

'I don't want to talk about it.'

'Somebody found Jakobson's body and decided to put it into the boot of your car, is that what you think?'

'Could be.'

'Sort of thing Totty Sweetman might have done, do you think?'

'Sweetman had no reason to do that to me.'

'Are you sure about that? No, of course you're not. Sweetman was at the Monkes Tale that night, wasn't he?'

'Yes.'

'Did you speak to him?'

'He spoke to me in the car park.'

'What did he say?'

'He wanted to know what I was doing there and I told him I just happened to be passing.'

'You didn't tell him you were meeting Ron Hitching?' Gino shook his head.

'What were you trying to find out from Hitching?'

'Ian wanted me to talk to him.'

'I know, you said that before, but talk to him for what purpose?'

'Ian thought it funny that Billy Cox was on the scene when the police got there.'

'Ian's not the only one.'

'He thought Ron Hitching could say why and that it'd help get him off his case.'

'You told me last time that Hitching suddenly panicked and refused to talk.'

'That's right.'

'What made him panic?'

'We were sitting in his car in a side road and suddenly another car pulled up in front and turned its headlights full on us.'

'Yes?'

'Then it drove off.'

'Who was the driver?'

'We never saw.'

'But you had your suspicions?'

'Yes. We were certain it was either Sweetman or Cox.'

'Where was your own car all this time?'

'I'd left it in the Monkes Tale car park.'

'So that anyone could have put Jakobson's body into the boot?'

'Yes.'

'It must have been Sweetman, mustn't it?'

'Could have been.'

'I'd say "was".' Patrick frowned. 'But he must have had a reason for doing it, mustn't he, Gino? You still haven't told me everything.'

'It could have been Sweetman's way of telling me to eff off.'

'Not to talk to Ron Hitching?'

'Something like that.'

Patrick could not help noticing the way Gino sought refuge in evasion every time they approached the crux question, namely, precisely what he was hoping to find out from Hitching. Moreover, he couldn't for the moment see why Gino should always stall at this particular point. A vital piece of the puzzle was still missing.

Two, perhaps, of which Gino was in possession of only one. In which event, Ron Hitching must be in possession of the other. It was therefore important to find Hitching without delay and he decided to give up his evening to that end.

It was only as he was going up to his office that he wondered how he was going to break the news to Jennie.

In fact he need not have worried, for when he called her home, Mrs King informed him that Jennie was spending the evening with a distant cousin who had unexpectedly turned up from Australia. Moreover, she told him before he had an opportunity of giving her the reason for his own call and in a tone which was obviously intended to mitigate his disappointment.

'How long is he over here for?' Patrick enquired politely.

'For a year. He's studying at an engineering college. I'll tell Jennie you called, Pat. I'm sure she'd love to go out another evening.'

Patrick grinned as he replaced the receiver. Undeserved credit didn't always have to be disclaimed.

*　　　　*　　　　*

Ian Tanner and Gail travelled home together in a brittle silence. He had scarcely addressed a word to her since they had left court. She knew that her appearance in the witness-box had been a near disaster and that he was furious with her, though heaven knows what he'd expected of her evidence.

After she had left the box, Mr Ridge had addressed the jury at inordinate length until everyone's expression had become glazed with boredom verging on despair. The jury at whom his closing speech was directed were in the unfortunate position of having to affect some sort of attention. Matthew Chaytor had the impression that they had drawn lots to listen two at a time, for while the majority always appeared to be sunk in impassive gloom, there were invariably a couple of jurors who managed to display a degree of alertness.

By the time Mr Ridge had exhausted his repertoire of legal clichés and had dealt with the evidence with all the finesse of a lion chewing a hunk of meat, the clock on the court-room wall showed ten minutes to four and the judge decided everyone had suffered enough for one day. After ascertaining that Andrew Batchford would be happier to make his final speech without a break, he adjourned the trial until the next morning, with a confidently expressed view to the jury that it would be their last day.

After a Tube journey, followed by a bus ride, Ian Tanner and Gail set off on the final two hundred yards' walk to her flat. Both the train and the bus had been crowded which had inhibited Gail from talking about what was uppermost in both their minds. As they walked the last stretch, however, she broke their silence.

'I'm sorry, Ian, if you think I let you down.'

'Forget it!' he said grimly.

'I was much more nervous than I expected to be.'

'You were terrible.'

'The judge felt sorry for me, anyway,' she said in a spirited tone.

'Fat lot of good that does me!'

'It might have been better if you'd ever told me the truth of what happened.'

'Do we have to go over that again?'

'Well, you never have, have you?'

'I don't see what difference it'd have made to your giving evidence.'

'At least I could have judged that for myself.'

'Look, Gail, lay off me, will you, please! I've got enough problems without your nagging.'

She bit her lip. 'What problems?' she asked in a puzzled voice.

'Only going off to prison tomorrow, that's all,' he said savagely.

'Mr Batchford thought it'd only be a fine or a suspended sentence,' she said with a slight catch in her voice.

'You made such a muck of your evidence, the judge'll probably put me inside. You made me sound like a liar with all your stammering and uncertainty.'

Gail was shocked into silence by the monstrous unfairness of the suggestion that, if Ian went to prison, it would be her fault. Luckily they had only a few yards to go to her door.

Suddenly a figure came toward them from the other side of the street. It was Gino Evans. Ian Tanner's jaw dropped when he saw him.

'I thought you were in the nick,' he said.

'They had to let me go. I hadn't done anything,' Gino replied with a touch of his old bravado.

'Where's your car?' Tanner asked, looking around.

'The police wouldn't let me have it back yet.'

While Tanner and Gino Evans mounted the staircase which ran at the side of the salon and led to Gail's flat, she went on a couple of yards and through the door of the salon itself.

It was crowded as it invariably was during the last hour of business, mostly with girls who had slipped away from

197

work a bit early to have their hair done on their way home and to an evening out with their boy-friends. They were not the type of customer to call on Gail's service as a manicurist.

She walked through the salon to the small room at the back where Miss Partridge, the manageress, could usually be found having a cup of tea and a cigarette at this hour of the day.

'I shall be back tomorrow,' she said, in response to Miss Partridge's faintly hostile glance.

'Good. It's been very inconvenient having you away the last few days. It's all over is it? What happened to your boy-friend?'

'It'll finish tomorrow, but I don't have to go back. I gave my evidence this afternoon.'

'You don't sound altogether happy. Is anything the matter?'

Gail shook her head. She had never treated Miss Partridge as a confidante and had no desire to start now.

'I'm just a bit tired. I expect it's the aftermath of giving evidence. It was rather a strain, more so than I'd expected.'

'A night's rest should put that right.'

The telephone rang on Miss Partridge's desk and Gail took the opportunity to slip away.

Ian and Gino cast her a conspiratorial look as she entered the living-room. Neither of them said anything as she walked through to the kitchen and closed the door behind her.

'You don't think she mucked her evidence because she's miffed with you?' Gino asked.

'No, she wouldn't do that. Anyway, I reckon we're more or less washed up now. Once this is all over, I'm off.'

'Where'll you go?'

'Haven't decided.'

'Abroad?'

'Nah! Somewhere in England. At least I can speak the lingo here. I might go up North.'

'Have you told her?'

'Don't be daft! And don't you drop any hints neither! Anyway, if I'm fined, I'll have to skip. I haven't got any money to pay bloody fines. And if I had, I wouldn't.' He paused and then gave Gino an interested look. 'What about you? Are you going to stay in these parts?'

Gino shrugged. 'Don't know. Probably not. Better to move somewhere your face isn't known.'

'By the law and the likes of Totty Sweetman,' Tanner added. He was feeling more amiable toward Gino than he had for some time. He considered that Gino's own recent troubles with the law had gone some way to redressing the balance between them. 'We might go somewhere together. I reckon we could work as partners.'

But if he expected Gino to leap at the proposition, he was disappointed.

'I'm not through with the law yet and nor are you,' Gino said. 'Anyway, you're a bit too accident prone for my liking.'

'I bloody well am not.'

'It was Mick who kept us together. I'm beginning to think, too, that we were a bit big-headed in our ideas.'

Tanner glowered at him. 'If that's the way you feel, I wouldn't want you for a partner.'

'That's the way I feel, Ian.'

It wasn't that Gino was halfway to turning over a new leaf, just that for some time now he had come to see Tanner as a liability. As someone who was destined to spend the next decade of his life, and possibly longer, in and out of prison. And that wasn't the sort of person with whom he wished to ally himself, other than for an occasional evening's drinking.

'Does it mean you're not going to try and find Ron Hitching?'

Gino nodded. 'No point, now.'

'Not much there isn't! Don't forget I'm still on the hook!'

'You'll be off it by this time tomorrow and there's no chance of my finding Ron Hitching before then.'

'Supposing I'm further on it. Supposing I'm in the Scrubs by this time tomorrow?'

'You won't be.'

'But supposing. Are you just going to let me rot?' His tone had become querulously insistent.

'Of course not, but it's not going to happen that way,' Gino said with weary patience. The bloke's a bit unhinged, he thought. Always has been, perhaps, but now he's worse.

Meanwhile out in the kitchen, Gail slowly chopped a tomato for a salad she was preparing. Ian's attitude on the way home had merely confirmed what she had intermittently been aware of for some time. The writing on the wall had been clear enough, save that she had usually chosen to turn her back on it. Living with him had been like trying to tame a wild animal. In the end its natural instincts prevailed. One half of her would be almost relieved when the break came, but the other half already felt the onset of overwhelming desolation at the prospect.

Once his trial was over, the end could come suddenly and without warning. Of course, if he was sent to prison, he would probably still cling to her and even though she would know that this was no more than a calculated impulse on his part, she would continue to stand by him.

She felt tears beginning to trickle down her cheeks and she quickly seized a tissue to wipe them away. Her life with Ian had never been exactly fun, but life without him was going to be a wilderness of despair for a time.

She put the slices of tomato into a bowl and reached for an onion. If Ian found her crying, he could attribute it to the onion.

*   *   *

200

When Matthew Chaytor arrived home, his wife was on the telephone talking to the manageress of her health food shop. He waited impatiently for her to finish.

'Is Bramley still here?' he asked.

'He left about an hour and a half ago. He didn't call you as he said you'd still be in court.'

'Oh! What was the outcome of his visit?'

'He took a statement from Peter. What, I gather, you call a witness statement.'

'Where's Peter now?'

'He's gone out. He said he'd like some fresh air and I told him I thought that was a good idea.'

'How did he seem after Bramley's visit? Relieved?'

'Not noticeably so.' She passed her fingertips across her forehead. 'I wish we could get him to a doctor, Matt.'

'We can suggest it, but I don't imagine he'll take kindly to the idea. He certainly won't if it comes from me. Why don't you have a word with him?'

Philippa sighed. 'I don't think he listens to me very much any more. It's such an awful vista ahead, long silences punctuated by S.O.S.s when he's in trouble.'

'It's not an uncommon one for many parents these days.'

'That doesn't make it any better. I'm not just a parent in the abstract, I'm Peter's mother.'

Matthew Chaytor could think of no appropriate rejoinder and walked towards the door.

'I'm going to fetch myself a drink. Shall I get you one?'

It was about an hour later when Peter arrived home. He came straight into the living-room where his parents were sitting desultorily watching the end of a television current affairs programme.

'I've decided to go,' he said, without any preliminaries.

'You don't mean now, this evening?' Philippa said in a startled voice.

'Yes.'

'But where to, Peter?'

'I have to collect my things from the Monkes Tale.'

'But where'll you go then?'

'I've got friends. I shan't be sleeping out in the street,' he said in a faintly amused tone.

'Supposing the police want to get in touch with you?' his father broke in.

'I'll call you in a day or so. I'm not going to disappear for ever.'

He came across to his mother and gave her a peck on the cheek. Then with a nod to his father he turned to leave the room. He had reached the door when Matthew Chaytor spoke.

'Here, hold on a moment. You'd better have this.'

Peter turned. In his father's hand were two £10 notes. For a few seconds he just stared at the money, then, with a slight shrug of indifference, he took it and left the room.

A moment later they heard the front door slam.

CHAPTER EIGHTEEN

It was raining when Patrick left the station around seven o'clock that evening and drove to what was referred to in police records as Hitching's last known address. It was the address from which he had moved only twenty-four hours earlier.

The woman who answered the door looked at Patrick with dark suspicion when he asked after Hitching's whereabouts.

'He's not here,' she said in a hostile voice and made to close the door.

Patrick, however, had read her intentions and had stepped a pace forward to block her move.

'Where's he gone?'

'I'm not saying. It's none of your business. You're the second person round here today looking for him.'

Patrick frowned. 'In that case, it's probably more urgent than ever that you tell me where to find him. I'm a police officer.'

'Police?'

He nodded. 'Who was the other person?'

'Said he was a friend.'

'Was he stocky in build with curly hair and a beard, and was he wearing dark glasses?'

'Yes.'

'Then let's hope I find Ron before he does. What did you tell him?'

She licked her lips. 'I told him I didn't know Ron's address which I don't. Or I didn't then. All I knew was that he was staying somewhere in Wandsworth. I told him that because he said he was a good friend of Ron's and wanted to warn him about something that had happened.'

She shook her head in a puzzled manner. She was not a very bright-looking woman and was obviously confused by all these enquiries after her lodger.

'But do you know Ron's address now?'

'He called me this afternoon and told me but said I wasn't to tell a soul.'

Patrick was thoughtful for a moment.

'Do you like him?'

'He's always treated me well.'

'You wouldn't want anything to happen to him?'

'No.'

'Well, if you don't tell me where I can find him, something may. That man who called here earlier was no friend of Ron's. If he gets to Ron before I do, it'll be a case of poor old Ron!'

It was obvious from her expression that Ron had uttered similar sentiments when she had told him on the phone of Billy Cox's visit.

'How do I know you're not going to arrest him and put him inside?'

'I'm not, but, even if I were, it would be better for him than being found by the other chap.'

'You look sort of all right,' she said, doubtfully. 'I only want to do what's best for Ron. Mind you, don't get ideas, I'm a respectable married woman even if my husband is in the Merchant Navy. Ron's my lodger and there's nothing between us.'

'But you still wouldn't want to attend his funeral?'

Her eyes opened in alarm. 'You don't mean . . . ?'

'I do,' Patrick broke in quickly, 'so you'd better tell me where I can find him and save his life.'

'Oh my God!' she muttered. She fetched a small scrap of paper from the pocket of her cardigan. 'It's Quinford

Street, number sixteen,' she said, reading with difficulty. 'I just hope I'm doing the right thing.'

'Don't worry, you are!' Patrick said in an encouraging tone, as he turned to get back into his car.

Quinford Street was tucked away on the north side of the district's main thoroughfare. It was ill-lit and consisted of small terraced Victorian villas. At one end there were a builder's yard and a monumental mason with samples of his work in a tiny open enclave adjoining his premises. At the farther end was a cluster of small shops.

Number 16 was at the end of the terrace and diagonally across the street from the monumental mason. No sign of light came from any of its windows.

All this Patrick gleaned as he drove the length of the street on a quick reconnaissance.

He decided to park his car round the corner to avoid arousing suspicion and to walk back to the house. It was still raining and there was a cold wind so that the roads were generally empty of pedestrians. Indeed, Quinford Street itself was not only deserted, but most of its houses appeared darkened. Either its residents were out or they lived in their back parlours.

A passage ran down the blind side of number 16 and Patrick decided to reconnoitre the rear of the house. There was a tiny yard with a high brick wall separating it from the property which backed on to it from the neighbouring street. A lean-to shed occupied one side of the yard and against the wall was a narrow strip of what he supposed was a garden, though it was difficult to envisage anything growing there with any enthusiasm.

The windows at the back of the house were similarly dark and it seemed clear that no one was at home. He nevertheless decided to put this to further test. There was a back door on which he knocked. There was no response. Next he peered through a window beside the door into what was apparently a small scullery. He could make out a sink and, over in a corner, what looked like a cooker.

He walked back down the passage and paused just before coming out on to the pavement. A glance at his watch told him that it was a few minutes after nine. It seemed reasonable to suppose that Ron Hitching was at one of the pubs in the neighbourhood. He might even be farther afield, up in the West End, for example, or have gone to keep a rendezvous with someone. But Patrick doubted this. If Hitching had gone to ground, the odds were that, for a couple of days or so, he wouldn't stray very far from his new abode. Animal instinct would keep him close to his burrow.

Patrick decided that nothing would be lost if he went off and gave himself a drink, as long as he didn't stay away too long. He had noticed a pub about a quarter of a mile away and, leaving his car where it was, set off on foot.

Both bars were crowded and he had to elbow his way through to buy a drink.

'A small Scotch please,' he said to the barmaid, a short, black-haired, hatchet-faced woman who looked as if she could quell a disturbance as easily as pull a pint of beer. She handed him his change and moved quickly to serve another customer. Patrick added a squirt of soda to his whisky and eased himself away from the bar.

There was no sign of Ron Hitching and he moved to where he could see into the other bar, but again without recognising anyone. He manoeuvred himself against a wall where he could stand without being constantly jostled by people beating a path to and from the bar. Inevitably he attracted a few glances from the regulars who spotted an unfamiliar face as quickly as if there was water in their beer.

He became aware of a girl pushing her way toward him. She was blonde and wore a low-cut black blouse that was having trouble containing her breasts.

'Why don't you join me and my friend?' she said with a leer. 'Don't like drinking on your own, do you?'

'I'm just going,' Patrick said.

The girl looked at him doubtfully as if trying to assess the truth. Then apparently deciding he was worth one more try, she said, 'Not in a hurry, are you, darling?'

'I'm afraid so.'

'Don't you like girls?'

Patrick could think of several answers to this, but, for the sake of a peaceful getaway, refrained from voicing any of them. Pushing his way past the girl, he put his empty glass on a table and made for the exit. On his way he glanced toward the blonde girl's companion who was sitting over in a corner. Her expression was one of secret amusement and he guessed that the approach had been a bet between them, which the blonde girl had lost.

The rain had let up slightly, but, from the look of the sky, could come down heavily again at any moment. He turned up his coat collar and walked off in the direction of Quinford Street.

It was as deserted as it had been half an hour earlier and there was still no sign of life at number 16. He had already decided that he would hang on at least until the pubs had closed and then, if there was still no sign of Ron Hitching, consider what his next move should be. He had also decided exactly where he would keep his watch.

Stepping over the low wall into the monumental mason's small yard, he positioned himself behind a solid granite headstone. It bore an inscription, but Patrick was quite glad that he was unable to read in the dark. He sent up a small prayer of gratitude, however, to his unknown benefactor. There was a small block of rough stone immediately behind it and he was able to sit on this with the headstone in front of him as a solid shield.

The rain had started to come down again and he crouched even lower, pulling his head down inside his collar. Large drops splashed on to the stoneware around him and bounced back at him.

A dull, uncomfortable and wholly uneventful forty minutes passed. Twice he stood up to stretch his limbs and shake himself like a dog.

He had just settled down again after the second occasion when he heard footsteps on the further pavement. Peering round the side of the headstone, he saw a figure moving past the builder's yard and approaching the passage which ran down the side of number 16.

Any moment now, the figure would pass beneath one of the few street lamps.

Yes, he was almost sure it was Ron Hitching. Moreover, a not entirely sober Ron Hitching from his slightly swaying gait.

He decided to remain behind his cover until he had seen Hitching enter the house. Then he would go across and beat on the door.

Hitching had just drawn level with the passage when a small van appeared from nowhere and came to a sudden, sharp halt beside him. A man leapt from the driver's seat and tore round the back of the van. It seemed to Patrick that with one hand he opened the back of the van while his other grabbed Hitching and jerked him backwards.

There was a muffled shout and Hitching seemed to sink to his knees. By this time, however, Patrick was halfway across the road. He reached the van as Hitching was being manhandled into the back.

Taking hold of Hitching's nearest leg, he wrenched him away from the van.

He heard an angry grunt from Billy Cox, whom he now recognised as the driver of the van, as Ron Hitching slumped into the gutter.

There was a sudden shot followed by a yell of pain and then the van tore off down the street.

For a second, Patrick stood stunned, unsure whether

he'd been hit, even whether it was he who had let out the yell. Then he bent down beside the prostrate Hitching and felt his pulse, which seemed to be beating strongly. With a feeling af relief he stood up again. He could see people opening doors and peering cautiously up and down the street. A few seconds later, he heard the sirens of approaching police cars.

There was nothing like a shot ringing out in the night to bring the police post haste to a scene of trouble, he reflected with gratitude.

CHAPTER NINETEEN

It was six o'clock the next morning before Patrick arrived home. Too late to think of going to bed, as he would have to be up again an hour later.

It was a relief, however, to get out of his clinging wet and mud-spattered clothes and lie in a hot bath for half an hour. Afterwards he shaved, made himself a cup of coffee and, wrapped in a dressing-gown, sat in a chair in his bedroom. He was tempted to stretch out on his bed, but knew that, if he did so, the odds were he would fall fast asleep and feel much worse when the alarm roused him than if he hadn't slept at all.

As he looked back over the long night's events, he found it difficult to realise they belonged to the same time sequence.

He had insisted on accompanying Ron Hitching in the ambulance which took him to hospital and had breathed a great sigh of relief on learning that he was suffering from nothing worse than a flesh wound in his right upper arm. The young casualty officer who had examined and dressed it recommended that he should remain in hospital overnight. Unless anything unforeseen occurred, however, the doctor was sure he'd be able to leave the next day.

When Patrick asked if he could interview him as soon as the doctor had finished, faces were pulled and demurring sounds were made. It was not unusual in such circumstances for medical and police interests to find themselves in conflict. Sometimes severe and highly recriminatory conflict. The fact that this didn't happen on this occasion was due as much to Patrick and the young casualty officer being of the same generation as to the relative slightness of the wound.

While he was waiting to be allowed to see him, Patrick made a long telephone call to Detective Inspector Shotter, as well as explaining the position to the officers who had arrived at the scene.

He had just finished speaking to D.I. Shotter when the casualty officer came in and said, 'You can talk to him now, but not for more than ten minutes. He needs a good night's rest and you'll be able to talk as long as you want tomorrow.' He paused and added, 'Are you sure you can't wait till then?'

'I'll be grateful for ten minutes now, Dr Renton. An awful lot of events tomorrow are going to hinge on what I can find out from Hitching tonight.'

'Very well, I'll take you to him.'

Patrick was not to know that one of the factors in his favour was calling the casualty officer by his name. If there was one thing Christopher Renton detested, it was being addressed as 'doc' by all and sundry.

Patrick found Ron Hitching in a side ward. He was propped up by a mound of pillows and his injured arm lay bandaged outside the bedclothes.

He looked at Patrick without recognition and with a faintly puzzled frown.

'I'm Detective Constable Bramley,' Patrick said with a small smile. 'We met in the gutter a couple of hours ago, but it wasn't the moment for introductions.'

'Was it you who got me away from Billy?'

'Yes.'

'He tried to get me into the van. He had something in his hand he tried to put over my face.'

Patrick nodded. 'A pad of chloroform. He dropped it in the road when he fled.'

'Who fired the gun?'

'Billy Cox.'

Hitching appeared to digest this information for a while before speaking again.

212

'Did he mean to shoot me?'

'What do *you* think?'

'He must have meant to kill me.'

'That's my bet, too.'

'I knew he was looking for me. That's why I left home.'

'I think you can count yourself lucky to be alive after this evening's events, Ron. If I'd not been on the scene, he'd have had you in that van and by now you'd most likely be fitted out in the latest style of concrete wear. As it was, your luck held still further when he only managed to wing you. A few inches to the left and he'd have scored a bull's eye.' As he spoke, Patrick jabbed a finger at his heart.

Hitching turned his head away and stared at the white hospital wall. Patrick now noticed an abrasion on the side of his chin. Nevertheless for someone who had been nearly kidnapped and then shot at, he looked in reasonable shape. He wasn't even showing any signs of a hangover and presumably had not been as drunk as he had appeared. Either that or the evening's events had had a sobering effect, as well they might.

Patrick tapped his foot lightly on the floor in a gesture of impatience. He couldn't afford to let any of his precious ten minutes seep away while Hitching stared at the wall with an unpractised air of meditation.

A few seconds later, however, he turned his head back and looked at Patrick.

'What do you want to know?' he asked, reluctantly.

'I want to know what really happened in Waterworks Lane the night Tanner killed Mick Burleigh?'

Hitching nodded slowly. 'It's been worrying me ever since it happened.' He took a deep breath. 'It's time the truth came out.'

CHAPTER TWENTY

At a quarter to ten Patrick made his way along the now well trodden judges' corridor. He had telephoned Judge Chaytor earlier that morning to say that there had been another development which he ought to know about before the trial was resumed.

'Does it affect my son?' the judge had asked warily. Patrick could detect a note of relief in his voice when he assured him that it did not.

'Good morning, Bramley,' Matthew Chaytor said as Patrick entered the room. 'I've never met a case which has been so full of untoward events. What is it this time?'

'I think you should be ready for a shock, sir.'

'Another?'

For the next ten minutes, he listened in attentive silence while Patrick told him what had happened the previous evening and of his hospital interview with Ron Hitching. When Patrick finished he shook his head in astonishment.

'It's as if we've been participating in a charade,' he said. 'A charade in which hardly one witness who mattered has told the truth. Heaven knows, one is used to perjury in the criminal courts, but, in view of what you now tell me, it is all too clear that this trial has been manipulated from start to finish.' He paused. 'Finish! Where does it finish? It seems to me that I have only two possible courses. One is to direct the jury to acquit, the other to discharge them from reaching a verdict and leave the police and the Director of Public Prosecutions to sort out the mess at their leisure. From a practical point of view it probably won't make much difference to Tanner, as even if I adopt the second alternative, I don't envisage anyone deciding to take the matter further against him. The charge of causing death by reckless driving has gone, anyway, though he could, I suppose, still be prosecuted for ordinary dangerous driving on the evidence of the panda-car drivers. As to the other charge I was proposing to sum up in his favour in view of Jakobson's unsatisfactory evidence. Not, let me add, that I have any sympathy with him. He more than brought the whole thing on his own head and then compounded the confusion with his own contribution of evasion and falsehood. It's hard to think of anyone who emerges from the whole sorry story with any credit at all. That is, saving yourself. I hope that your part in disentangling the truth will receive proper recognition.' Judge Chaytor got up and walked over to the window and stared out. It was two or three minutes before he turned round and said, 'I think that it'll be best if I discharge the jury, as I really don't feel disposed to direct them to acquit in all the circumstances. I obviously can't say too much in open court for fear of prejudicing future proceedings, but I must give them some sort of explanation for abandoning the trial at this eleventh hour. Before I do that, however, I think both counsel are entitled to hear what you've told me and I propose to send for them to come along to my room. You wouldn't mind going over it for their benefit, would you?'

'No, sir.'

'It'll come much better from you, than second-hand from me.'

He pressed a bell and, when an usher appeared, gave the necessary instructions.

While they were waiting for Bruce Ridge and Andrew Batchford to appear, he said, 'I haven't told you that my son left home yesterday evening. He said he'd keep in touch, but that's no guarantee that he will. I suppose he may be required as a witness at the inquest on Jakobson?'

'Yes, sir.'

'Well, that's a difficulty that'll have to be met if and when it arises.' In a tired voice he went on, 'I had hoped that his experiences at the Monkes Tale might have re-shaped his outlook, but I suppose that was hoping for an easy miracle. I think Peter's only hope is to fall under the influence of some strong-minded, sensible girl who will have the urge and the strength to stand him up on his feet and keep him from collapsing. They do exist, one believes, and it may be Peter's luck to meet one.'

There was a knock on the door and Batchford and Ridge came in. They were robed for court and sat down at the judge's invitation.

'This somewhat chequered trial has now received a final knock-out,' Judge Chaytor observed. 'Detective Constable Bramley will explain.'

Andrew Batchford had raised a quizzical eyebrow on seeing Patrick in the judge's room, while a frown of faint disapproval had flickered across Mr Ridge's face, as if he had come across the gardener sitting with his feet up in the drawing-room.

Patrick took a deep breath and began. 'Last night Cox, who you'll remember was a prosecution witness in this case, attempted to kidnap a man named Hitching. When his attempt was foiled he fired a shot at him with the obvious intention of killing him.'

'I think I should interrupt to say that the fact the kidnap attempt was foiled was entirely due to Bramley,' the judge said.

Andrew Batchford looked at Patrick with new interest, but Mr Ridge's frown merely deepened.

'Is Cox now in custody?' he asked.

'No, but he will be as soon as we find him. A man named Sweetman, who, we suspect, was his accomplice, has been brought in for questioning, but so far he's refusing to say anything. It's only a matter of time before we arrest Cox.

'Sweetman, Cox and Hitching were members of the same gang at the time your client, Mr Batchford, took Jakobson's car last September. It so happened that Hitching was courting Mick Burleigh's sister then and police learnt later through the grapevine that as a result of what happened that night he had begun to put distance between himself and Sweetman and Cox.' He paused and glanced at the two counsel. 'I know Mr Batchford has never felt that this trial has produced the truth of what really happened and how right he is. The idea of Tanner having taken the car for a joy-ride seemed implausible, but in default of any other explanation it was all we had.

'According to Hitching, who has made a long statement in hospital, Tanner, Burleigh and a man named Gino Evans reckoned to cock a snook at Sweetman and his friends because they'd been left smarting after the two factions had clashed earlier in the year. It seems that Sweetman's lot warned them to keep out of their way and not to tangle with the big boys. In effect, they were told that they were only fit to pilfer children's sweets.

'After Jakobson had gone off to Spain on holiday last autumn, it came to the ears of Tanner and his friends that the Sweetman gang had planned some job, for which they were proposing to use Jakobson's car. What sweeter, they thought, than to take the car themselves and spike their opponents' plan.

'Unfortunately, Burleigh became increasingly nervous about the whole idea and apparently in the hope that it could be peaceably thwarted, he told Hitching what was afoot. As I've said, Hitching was courting Burleigh's sister at the time and was in and out of the Burleigh house most evenings. He also seems to have got on well with Mick Burleigh. However, as a loyal member of the Sweetman gang he relayed the news to his colleagues, who were far from amused and determined this time to teach Tanner and his friends a lesson they wouldn't forget.

'All they knew, however, was that Jakobson's car was to be nicked before they could get their own hands on it. They didn't know what Tanner's lot were proposing to do with it. So the night before it happened, they abducted Burleigh and tortured him until he told them of the plan to abandon it in the wood at the end of Waterworks Lane.

'According to Hitching, Burleigh was more dead than alive when they'd finished with him. Incidentally, Hitching strenuously denies that he had anything to do with this part of it and, indeed, that it was his disgust at what Cox and Sweetman did to Burleigh that caused him to break away and eventually to talk. On the evening in question, Sweetman and Cox took the unfortunate Burleigh to Waterworks Lane and hid there until they heard the car coming. It was a ten to one chance that it was either Tanner or Evans in Jakobson's car, as the lane was virtually unused by traffic at night. As the car came round the bend they propelled Burleigh into its path.

'What they didn't know was that Tanner was being chased by a police panda car. The result was that Cox was caught at the scene ostensibly in the role of Good Samaritan, but in reality bending over the body to make sure Burleigh was dead. Sweetman was able to get away unseen.'

'What an appalling story!' Andrew Batchford remarked. 'I imagine that if you can corroborate some of what Hitching has told you, Sweetman and Cox will both face murder charges?'

'I hope so, sir.'

'It's about as callous a crime as I've ever come across.' He turned to the judge. 'Meanwhile, what are you proposing to do about my client, judge?'

'I shall discharge the jury and leave others to sort out the mess.'

'You wouldn't consider directing them to acquit? It would be preferable for Tanner.'

'I'm sure it would, not that I feel he merits any sort of preferential treatment. But if I did that, I'd have to tell the jury much more than I properly can in open court. Indeed,' he went on, 'everything we've heard in this room is hearsay and quite inadmissible from an evidential point of view.'

Andrew Batchford smiled. 'Don't worry, judge, I'm not going to press you. I just felt I ought to make the right noises on my client's behalf. Incidentally, do I now gather that Jakobson died of natural causes?'

'Yes.'

'Then what was he doing in the boot of someone's car?'

'Jakobson died of a heart attack,' Patrick broke in when the judge looked faintly embarrassed. 'Sweetman and Cox found his body and put it into the boot of Evans' car. They'd begun to get a bit worried about Hitching avoiding them and that evening their fears about his loyalty were confirmed when they saw him and Evans together.'

Andrew Batchford gave a bemused shake of the head. 'Talk about oak trees growing from acorns!'

Mr Ridge remained silent, his lips pursed in an expression of frowning gravity.

'Incidentally,' Andrew Batchford went on, 'why did Jakobson give so much away under cross-examination? He agreed with practically everything I put to him?'

'I don't think it was anything more than wishing to be all things to all people. He was obviously apprehensive about giving evidence. I suspect he was worried that he might be asked awkward questions about his own activities, so he decided to disarm you by agreeing with everything you said. After all, it didn't really matter to him if Tanner was acquitted.'

'But wasn't he in danger of incurring Sweetman's wrath by giving Tanner a let-out, at least on the one charge?'

'Jeff Jakobson was used to wheeling and dealing. And anyway I'm not sure that Sweetman was so interested in the outcome of the case. He'd made his point when Tanner was charged with causing Burleigh's death by reckless driving.'

Mr Ridge now broke his reproving silence. In a somewhat censorious tone, he said, 'I'm surprised that the pathologist completely failed to distinguish between the different injuries Burleigh received. I should have expected him to have spotted that some of them had been caused by being beaten up.'

The judge and Andrew Batchford stared at him in mild surprise.

'I think you're being wise after the event,' Batchford said. 'All he was concerned with was a body which he'd been told had been struck by a fast-moving car. The injuries he found were consistent with that. It was a straightforward case of death on the road and he had no reason to suspect otherwise.

The judge nodded. 'I'd have thought, too, that the beating-up injuries could well have merged with the others. After all, they were not dissimilar types of treatment so far as their effect on the body was concerned. Just a matter of degree.' He glanced at his watch. 'If we're not to keep everyone waiting, it's time to get into court.'

As Patrick went to follow the two advocates out, he heard the judge call him back.

'I'm grateful to you for not bringing Peter's name into your account,' he said quietly as Patrick turned.

CHAPTER TWENTY-ONE

Patrick glanced round the familiar scene as he waited for the judge's entry. The twelve jurors had been emboldened by their three days of service and propinquity into exchanging nods and whispered words. Ian Tanner was sitting in the dock with his usual scowl, resentful and suspicious of his surroundings. His eyes met Patrick's and moved quickly on.. The usher, the official shorthand-writer and the clerk of the court all in their usual places. All of them waiting for the curtain to rise like an audience which knows the play backwards.

Patrick found it difficult to realise that this was where, for him, it had all started three days earlier. He recalled somewhat wryly his complete absence of interest in the case as he'd sat in court the first morning. Was it really only three days ago?

Three knocks on the door at the back of the bench heralded the judge's arrival and everyone stood up. The usual bows were made and everyone settled down, as Judge Chaytor turned to face the jury.

'Members of the jury, I very much regret to tell you that your time on this trial has been wasted as I'm about to discharge you from returning a verdict. There has been a certain development overnight which makes it quite impossible to continue the trial. I'm afraid I can't tell you very much because, by doing so, I might prejudice action which will have to be considered in other quarters in the coming days. All I will say is that something has arisen which casts the gravest doubt on evidence given in this court by one of the prosecution's witnesses. In those circumstances, I have no alternative but to discharge you

223

now, to thank you for your conscientious attention during the trial and to repeat once more my regret that your time has been wasted.' He turned and looked at Tanner who was nudged into standing up by a prison officer. 'I shall release you on bail formally to await re-trial, though whether any further trial will in fact take place will be for others to decide. Do you understand?'

'It's not fair,' Tanner said angrily. 'You ought to tell the jury to acquit me. If the prosecution witnesses have all lied, they have to let me off. I want to protest,' he added, as the prison officer tried to motion him into silence.

Matthew Chaytor looked at defending counsel. 'You will doubtless explain the position to your client, Mr Batchford?'

'Indeed, my lord.'

A few minutes later, the court was emptying against the background murmurs of extravagant speculation. Patrick and Andrew Batchford were the last two left.

'You must be feeling rather pleased with yourself,' Andrew Batchford remarked with a smile. When Patrick grinned, he added, 'If you remember, I told you there was more to this case than met the eye?' Patrick nodded. 'It hasn't been an easy one for the judge either. I've not come across him before. Seems a sane, sensible sort of man, which is more than one can say for some of them. Somebody did tell me that he had a son who'd caused him a bit of trouble, but I wasn't told in what way.'

Patrick put on an expression of polite interest, but said nothing. His mind was already wrestling with the more immediate problem of how to woo Jennie *and* stay in the police.

H | '93   94   13
      11   11

NO RENEWALS!

PLEASE RETURN BOOK AND REQUEST
AGAIN.